THE WORLD
from the
EYE OF A CHILD

THE WORLD
from the
EYE OF A CHILD

WRITTEN AND ILLUSTRATED BY

DWIJA VASHISHT

PARTRIDGE
A Penguin Company

ISBN: Hardcover   978-1-4828-0064-7
               Softcover   978-1-4828-0065-4
               Ebook   978-1-4828-0063-0

Partridge books may be ordered through booksellers or by contacting:

Partridge India
Penguin Books India Pvt.Ltd
11, Community Centre, Panchsheel Park, New Delhi 110017
India
www.partridgepublishing.com
Phone: 000.800.10062.62

Contents

CHAPTER-1

The Discovery

"T hump"

"Thump"

I opened my eyes and looked around. Where was this sound coming from? I looked around my pink-walled room. My elder sister, Neha, was sleeping peacefully in her side of the bed. She doesn't seem very dangerous when she is sleeping. She looks pretty. But trust me, when she is awake she seems nothing less than a monster to me.

"Thump"

I decide to get up and see what this is. I looked at the hello-kitty clock on my bedside table, it was 3am at night. It's probably mummy or papa up for a glass of water. But what if . . . what if it's a thief? I decided to go and look. I cautiously got out of my bed. The floor was freezing cold. But then, what else do you expect on a cold December night? I bundled up even tighter in my pink, furry blanket. Wrapping it around me like a shawl, I made up my mind. With one last look at my sister, I took small, nervous steps to the kitchen. My feet started to tremble. Maybe I should just wake up mummy or papa. After all, they are stronger and fearless too.

On the dim yet brighter side, if I really do catch the thief or whatever that source of sound is, I will be the heroine. Just for once, I will be the center of attention, not my *Perfect Sister*. Who is, like always, the centre of attention. Her good marks and good life make her the perfect role model for me. How many times I had wished I was like her. Naturally, she was the apple of my parent's eyes. "What do you want for dinner, Neha?" or "Neha, I am proud of you." No one ever asks me. It is all about Neha, all the time. No one ever says, "Nitya, which restaurant will we eat in today?" or "Nitya, we are so proud of you." These details may seem insignificant and make me seem like a problematic child but in a 7 year old's life, getting to choose the restaurant or being able to order from the menu is the most important thing in our lives at the moment.

"Thump"

The sound was definitely louder this time. It was surely coming from the kitchen. I started to walk faster. I was standing just outside the kitchen door now. Should I open the door? But for once, my thoughts overwhelmed me. I wasn't thinking rationally. I was not thinking about the thief, but about how I would be the favourite child. I didn't care about how dangerous this task was, I wanted to do it. Maybe it really wasn't a thief; it was just a rat or something but I wanted to prove myself anyway. My sister would be just sitting there, all jealous. I opened the door and peered inside. My heart was beating so fast I thought it's going to pop out any second. But luckily, it didn't.

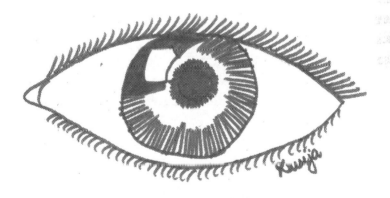

The first thing I saw in the dark, wood-paneled kitchen were two magical green eyes glowing back at me. Oh My God! There is **Voldemort**[1] in my kitchen, stealing some chocolate-chip cookies and milk. Before I could stop and think about what was going on, I let out a scream just like in the horror films my sister watches. Then the world blacked out. Voldemort had done it again.

I couldn't believe it. I wasn't dead, I had just fainted. Looks like Voldemort felt some pity for the person from whose kitchen he stole his cookies from. I had woken up when I felt something cold being sprinkled on my face. I opened my eyes to see Didi staring at me. Her brown hair was sprawled across her face. I would have laughed and made fun of her appearance, but I don't know why I let the chance slip. Good, now I had woken *her* up. Way to be a heroine Nitya. But she wasn't laughing at me. She looked . . . worried. Worried about me, I suppose. Or maybe wishing she had taken Voldemort's autograph first. She looked so scared that I got even more scared than I already was.

Elder Sibling Rule #45: *Elder siblings are mysterious creatures. They are the most vulnerable and defenseless*

---

[1] **Voldemort:** A fictional character and the main antagonist of J. K. Rowling's *Harry Potter* series. He is also a sadist who hurts and murders people—especially Muggles—just for pleasure. He has no conscience, feels no remorse, and does not recognize the worth and humanity of anybody except himself.

when they have just woken up. Use this to your advantage.

The "Elder Sibling Rulebook", conceptualized by me, contains many tips and tricks on how to live, and survive, with an elder sibling. I keep referring to these rules once in a while, whenever needed.

I looked at her. I sat up and looked around. Everything was normal. The glass dining table, the dark mahogany wood chairs, the white walls, the lavender curtains and my *'DIDI'*.

"What happened here?" I asked. I decided to give time for Voldemort to run away.

"I was sleeping when I heard a scream, I came to see who that was and I saw you lying flat outside the kitchen," she explained.

"I screamed? But was anybody there? Like a thief or someone?" I didn't explain more, Didi was already giving me quizzical looks.

"I was sleeping too and heard a noise. I thought it was a thief. So I got up and looked in the kitchen."

"There was no thief in the kitchen, silly! It must have been the cat or something! Don't get too worked up."

A Cat? **Professor McGonagall[2]**?

"Anyways, you were pretty brave! I wouldn't have gone out and looked if I ever heard such a noise. I would probably just tell mom about it. You deserve a treat!"

"Oh! Ok. Well to tell you the truth, I wasn't pretty brave myself. Didi, promise me something first?"

"What?" she said, irritated.

"That you wouldn't tell anybody about what happened today. Not even to any of your friends, not even mom or dad. I want you to keep it a secret."

"Of course I wouldn't tell anyone. It was real bravery though, what you did. But I think we should go to sleep now. It's pretty late else we'll wake mom or dad up. They'll put both of us in real trouble if they get to know what we are doing, up so late."

Elder Sibling Rule #89*: They never mean what they say. Never trust them if you value your life.*

---

[2]   **Professor McGonagall:** A character in the famous *Harry Potter* books who can change herself into her Animagus form of a British Shorthair silver tabby cat on will.

"Umm I guess. Let's go," I replied, I was feeling tired, now that the excitement is over.

Of course, my sister would never break any rules. Rules are meant to be broken. That's how the world goes. However, I didn't want to bother explaining that to her. I wasn't in a mood for a moral lecture.

Wow! My Didi actually cared. My sister did have a heart. *And that heart loved and cared for me, deep inside.* I always thought she didn't actually possess that vital organ.

I got to my bed and pulled the sheets up to my chin. Staring up at the glow-in-the-dark stars on the ceiling, I closed my eyes. I wasn't sleepy though. I was thinking about what had happened a few minutes ago. It wasn't Voldemort. Harry had killed him in the last movie. I remember how I had buried my face in a big tub of popcorn while my sister had watched the movie as if her life depended on it. I had agreed to go with her only if she bought me a large tub of caramel popcorn.

I had actually seen a cat. An ordinary cat. And her green, glowing eyes had scared me, causing me to faint.

When all this made sense, I felt foolish. I got scared by a cat's eye. I was thinking about being a heroine? I couldn't even fight a cat.

"Didi . . ."

"Yeah?" She sounded kind of groggy, like I had woken her up from a deep sleep. But she hadn't sounded groggy while she revived me. Looks like *that* was an angel. *This* one is my normal, everyday, tormenting sister. *Sigh* . . .

"Was I dumb, in the way I acted about a cat? But I couldn't help it. The cat's eyes were staring back at me." I blurted out before I could stop my tongue.

"No, you weren't dumb. You were very brave for a girl who is only 7 years old. Now go to sleep, will you?"

Is this angel here to stay or what?

"OK. But don't you think the cat had such a mysterious way of entering our house? I really want to see her again. Make her my pet."

"You can't make her a pet. She is a street cat. Do what you want to though, and let me go to sleep."

"What do we name her?" I asked, persistent for an answer.

"I told you, let me sleep! You are the one to think of a name for that weird ginger, black or whatever colored cat!" Didi looked like she wanted to get out of this conversation as soon as possible.

"Thanks for the name. *Ginger* sounds perfect."

"That's a weird name but I think we will be able to manage it. A weird girl with a cat with a weird name! Ha-ha!"

"I'm going to kill you!" I joked. But for once, I didn't feel bad about what she had said about me. After all, I know she means well. I hit her with my pillow. She grabbed another and a full on pillow fight erupted. At the end, our stomachs hurt from laughing so much. But it was worth it after all. *I realized that beneath all that perfume, my sister was sweet and caring.* I lay down on my bed and stared up at the ceiling. It seemed that my life was perfect. It was just the way I wanted it to be. The only thing I was worried about was whether or not Harry knew that Voldemort could transfigure into a Ginger cat.

CHAPTER-2

The New Normal

I woke up the next morning feeling super sleepy. My eyes looked all strange and puffy. My sister's eyes were the same too. I got up grudgingly and started to get ready for school.

I had already done all my homework the day before. I had to do some Maths assignments. Maths is my favourite subject. I always understand it, it's very logical. But everyone else seems to dislike it, which I don't understand. There was also this English chapter I had to read. It was about a girl who discovers a sparrow's nest on her window sill. The sparrow gives eggs and the girl becomes very good friends with the little baby sparrows that hatch from it. Yeah, like that's ever going to happen. I'm sure these kinds of things don't happen in real life. So why do they make stories out of it anyway?

I was putting my lunchbox in my bag when I suddenly saw Didi smiling at me. But it wasn't looking like a smile; it was more of a smirk. Looks like that angel has left. I looked at her and silently asked her why she was smiling at me. She pointed towards the kitchen and started to giggle. It was when I looked in the kitchen that I realized why she was smiling. It was my blanket, slippers and the glass of water Didi had used! I had left all of these things outside the kitchen. Mom knows that Didi has this habit of getting up at the slightest sound and drinking water. Her midnight feasts are more than just famous. But she knows I am a heavy sleeper. I couldn't blame her for thinking about why my blanket and slippers were lying outside the kitchen.

Elder Sibling Rule #75: *When they laugh, close your eyes and just RUN.*

"Stop laughing!" I whispered to Didi.

"But, it's so funny! Remember, you can't blame me . . . or your secret will accidently reach Mom's ears . . ."

"Nitya, what is your blanket doing here? I know you're a bit scared of the dark and you always wake me up when you want water, which you rarely do. So did you come in the night all by yourself? And why did you forget to take your blanket? Do you know how cold it is? What if you get sick?"

So. Many. Questions. Trust me, I never hear the end of these. What? Why? Where? When? That is what I hear every living moment of the day.

"Umm . . . well . . ." I stammered, thinking of a good excuse.

It was hard to say anything with Didi standing by your side, trying to stuff her laughter back in her mouth. But, as I could see, she wasn't doing a very good job of it. I could hear few giggles break loose.

"Neha! What's so funny? Did I crack a joke?"

Yay! Saved. Mom can focus on my sister's unexpected laughter and give me time to think of an excuse. But it is not going to last for long, I'm telling you! My mom can't bear to scold my sister for more than 42.42 seconds.

"Nothing Mom, Nothing."

I didn't want Didi to spill the beans. I had to make mom change the subject. Was telling mom about Voldemort's visit a good enough topic? I decided to drop that topic and focus on something more realistic and *'academic'*.

"Our school is taking part in an all India Maths quiz! It's going to be so much fun! There is going to be a quiz between all the 4 sections of our school first. Each section's team will comprise of 4 students. And the team that wins gets to compete with other schools of Delhi. The school level winner team gets to participate in the state level and then the national level quiz takes place. I really want to participate." I was breathless. The rules of the quiz were already way too complicated.

"That's amazing! Wow! That's a huge opportunity for you. You should definitely participate Nitya."

"Yes mom, I know. Tomorrow we will have a small Maths test to select the team for our section. I am going to give it a try."

"Nitya, don't you think we are getting late? We're going to miss the bus!"

Elder Sibling Rule #32: *Never steal their glory.*

Didi . . . spoils the moment for me, again. But to think about it, we *were* getting late.

"Oops . . . I totally forgot. Let's go. Bye mom!"

My dad leaves for work really early. I don't get to meet him most of the time when I am going to school. But mom is always at home when we leave for school. We have loads of fun with her.

At our bus stop, the bus screeched to a stop. I got in, followed by Neha. I found an empty seat and sat down. Didi sat down with one of her friends. I looked out of the window. People were rushing around, going to work or to school. There were many school buses, with children shouting, screaming or even sleeping!

So here it is; a new day and a new beginning.

CHAPTER-3

A Determined Thought

"Triiiinnnngggggg . . ."

The familiar school bell with which we are more than familiar with . . .

So here I am, sitting in my classroom. You know what? You can never get bored sitting in a classroom. There is always something going on. A game, fighting between people, singing a new **Bollywood**[3] song . . . and countless fun things. But it is not so fun when the teacher comes . . .

"Good morning, class! How are you all today? Fresh and ready to study, I hope!"

---

[3] **Bollywood:** The Indian entertainment industry. Similar to Hollywood.

Wow! It's like magic, one moment I am saying how boring class is when the teacher comes and she is here in front of me. Is there some kind of brain reading device in the teacher's lounge? Whenever the children are having the most fun, the teacher is supposed to enter and ruin it. A minute ago, I was having fun watching Divya and Natasha fighting about who had done a better project. Wait. I'll tell you who has a better one. None of them. They are not the ones who have made the project. It's their mothers who wake up the whole night making good projects for them. Yet they come to school and brag about what a beautiful project they have made. Hah! And to top it all, all the kids come swarming around then saying things like, "No! You both have made wonderful projects . . ." "I wish I could have a wonderful project as you have . . ." "You are so talented . . ." You can see them going red with pleasure and pride. None of which they deserve.

And yes! There were also these class toppers doing a sum from a fifth grade Maths book. I somehow don't know their names. Our class has around 50 students and we just had a class reshuffling at the start of the year. These two were always in some Maths book; I never really talked to them. Today was no different. They were solving some questions and they were fighting too, but about who had got the question right. How do they solve these questions, anyway? I am unable to solve a few of my own questions sometimes and they are already solving a fifth grade book! I mean, come on!

Oh! I got completely lost in my thoughts! Well then, where were we? Got it. The teacher was here. I am supposed to wish her now.

"Good morning ma'am."

We say that every day, don't we? I doubt anyone even means it, it's just one of those things you do subconsciously.

"Sit down kids. Let's start our lessons for the day. Has everyone finished the homework that was given to you yesterday?"

This sentence, too, is repeated in a classroom every day. It is then followed by the sound of opening bag packs and taking out of the notebooks. But everyday there are a group of people who come out with a "No ma'am. We didn't do our homework."

Why don't these people do their homework on time? Don't their parents tell them to do their homework? Mine would probably kill me if I didn't. "Do your homework!" I hear that so many times that it strikes in my ears. I feel it is better to humor them by doing my homework than to face the serious repercussions. It's not that I don't want to do it. I just don't want to do it *just* then.

It's time for the first period now, English. To tell you the truth, I am a bit scared of our English teacher. She is one of those strict teachers who constantly shout at the students. I like my Maths teacher though. She is very sweet and knows how to make us understand things. Once, we had to learn how to subtract. She made us get 10 toffees from home and then taught us by saying, "Eat 3 toffees." "Now keep 5 toffees away." "Now add 3 toffees to the remaining . . ." It was so much fun. We all got to eat 10 toffees during class. And the best part is that she teaches us in such an interesting way that even those kids who don't do their homework scored good marks in their subtraction test!

Uh oh! We are getting our test papers back today. You can actually feel the tension in the class. Our English teacher is known for strict marking. I waited till my roll number was called, fidgeting constantly. I wished someone would call her and she would leave for the rest of the class. I didn't want my paper. *She could keep it if she wants it so badly.*

"Roll number 26, 29 out of 30. Very good performance! You've got the highest in the whole class. Has your sister been tutoring you?"

Wow! I got 29 marks! I had studied so hard for this exam, I wasn't that surprised! I decided to ignore the last comment. My sister couldn't steal my glory now. I could see Divya and Natasha's eyes boring into my test paper. I seriously had the urge to go up to them and tell them that their mothers could not give their tests! Ha!

As happy as I was in the English period, the sadder I got in the Maths period. I found out that our Maths teacher has left the school! We were given a new teacher. She was good but no one can take the place of my favourite teacher. I could see how much she was trying to get us to like her. I decided to give her a chance, she seemed so sweet. Plus, I didn't want to spoil my lucky day. It was probably her lucky day too.

The whole day went routine for me. Our next period is supposed to be creative writing. We were given a topic and we had to write something on it. The teacher came to our class and wrote on the blackboard:

"Write a paragraph on the topic MY PET. If you don't own one you can assume that you do."

When I saw the topic I immediately thought about Ginger. During the happenings of the day I had totally forgotten about her. *Or him.* I had not seen her even once. How was I supposed to write about something that I haven't even seen once? And that also arose the curiosity for me to actually see what she looks like. I made up my mind to see her today if she visits our kitchen. I'll even leave some food and milk for her. Wait till I reach home and explain my plan to Neha Didi. Wait till she hears about my marks which I scored in English. I can't wait to see her fuming with jealousy. Right now though, the only thing on my mind was *'Ginger'*.

CHAPTER-4

An Unexpected Treat

"**M**om! *Listen* mom! I have great news for you!"

"Wait, wait! What is the hurry? I am coming!"

It was seven at night, my mother had just returned from work. Her face was flushed and tired. She seemed irritable. In short, *all was normal.*

"I scored 29 marks in my English paper. It's the highest in the whole class."

"Well done, Nuts." Guess who that was? Correct. *Obnoxious teenager sibling, was I even talking to you?*

Elder Sibling Rule #88: *Even if you are not, you are always talking to them.*

"That's very good! I am proud of you! You deserve a treat! Tell me what do you want to eat?" My mom's *my—child—has—done—well* speech is so familiar to me. These four sentences are they only things she ever says when someone does well. Didi can probably say them with her. Over the years, I have observed that not only do they look fake, but also rhyme.

I was listening to mom but I wasn't paying any attention to what she was saying. My mind was still thinking about Ginger. I heard the word 'eat' and without thinking, instantly replied, "Milk."

"Milk? I asked you what you wanted to eat, Nitya. Do you want a pizza or a burger? I am pretty sure you don't want milk!"

This was when I came back to my senses. I had to stop thinking about Ginger all the time. It's good to be excited about my very own pet cat but I didn't want to be completely lost. If I continued with this kind of thoughtful wanders, mom might get suspicious. Whenever she is suspicious, she goes and asks Neha about the matter. Neha would, naturally, spill her guts out. No, I had to be careful.

"I mean, milk chocolates mom, those ones they show on TV. I want to eat those," I replied, hastily.

Phew, saved by some quick thinking! Chocolate is something that is literally made by anything! You can always save yourself be adding chocolate to anything edible. Milk Chocolate, Coconut chocolate, Fruit n Nut chocolate . . . *now, let's not get carried away here!*

"Oh, OK. You want some milk chocolates, right? Here, I'll give you the money. You go to the market with Neha and buy them." She fiddled with her wallet. "Here you go. I've given you 100 rupees. That should be more than enough."

Well, I have to admit seeing that crisp and new 100 rupee note made me forget about Ginger in a jiffy. Money and fear makes people do crazy things . . .

"Oh thank—you Mom! You are the best!"

I gave her a hug and Didi and I raced off to wear our shoes and go to the market. I tried to tie my shoelaces fast, but all in vain. Didi threw on her bright red converses in a second.

"Hurry up, fatso! I want to go to the shop today itself!" Didi is always so sweet, isn't she? *This* is the reason I absolutely adore her.

Elder Sibling Rule #66: *Never be nice to them, it never work.*

"I'm coming! Help me tie my shoelaces please?"

"What's in it for me?" *Didi is always helpful. Kindness is her middle name.*

Elder Sibling Rule #59: *Kindness is their middle name. They are one of the most caring and unselfish people you will ever meet. Just thinking about them makes me want to cry.* ***sob*** . . .

"They are shoelaces, for heaven's sake! What could you possibly expect me to give you for tying them? Leave it; I'll do it on my own. Humph!" By that time, I had managed to tie them, though sloppily.

As we were walking along the road to the shop, I could see that Didi and I were both freezing. None of us had remembered to put jackets on. It was a small walk but neither of us wanted to run.

"You really don't want milk chocolates, do you?" Didi asked, her teeth chattering. *She looked like a goldfish with lip-gloss on.*

Umm . . . I told you about the mind reading device in the teachers' lounge, right? I suspect there is one in Didi's brain too. I think there is one is everyone's brain. I am the *only* exception. Didi always says that it's written on my face but I never believed her. Just as a precaution, I wiped my hand across my face. It came out clean.

"Huh? What makes you say that? I saw the advertisements for it and thought I'd very well try it."

Elder Sibling Rule #12*: Never tell them the truth. They get to know anyway, so why do the dirty task of telling them yourself and getting humiliated?*

"You were thinking about Ginger, weren't you? You can't hide anything from me. I'm your sister."

See? Can I do the **'I told you so' dance**[4] *now?*

I am not at all doubtful about the mind reading device now . . . I am sure there is one!

"Umm . . . Uh . . . I . . . Yes. I was thinking about her. But so what? And by the way, how do you know what I am thinking about? Do you have a mind-reading device? I am pretty sure now that it isn't written on my face, I just wiped it."

"Ha ha! What? Mind reading device? Are you totally nuts! I am your sister; I can sense what you are

---

[4]   **I told you so dance:** Whenever somebody tells something to another person which they don't believe and that is precisely what happens, that person is entitled to an 'I told you so dance' which involves a running man (a dance style in which a person is running but not moving from his/her position) and fist pumping the air. This dance is generally used as an insult.

thinking about. Your mind is like an open book to me. Now tell me what you want, we have reached the shop." I was a little glad that our talking made us reach the shop faster and not feel the cold.

"Um . . . anything would do. Now that you know, I actually hate milk chocolates. It's my treat, right, so I get to decide . . . let's do one thing, why don't we buy a chocolate cake mix? We can make the cake and surprise everyone!"

"Nice idea, lil sis!" she chirped. (Do goldfishes chirp?) I scowled. Ugh! I hate it when she calls me that.

"Let's go see the different flavours and prices. Remember, we only have a 100 rupee note." Didi continued speaking, pretending not to see me scowling at her. *She always ruins the good mood with her practicality. She should learn to LIVE.*

We started looking around the shop. I glanced at a shelf and saw a packet of chocolate cake mix. I picked it up and examined it. It was Rs. 149! I looked around but this was definitely the cheapest. The others were the ones with the eggs. This was definitely the cheapest eggless one. I ran to Didi to tell her.

"Didi, I've checked all of them. The cheapest I could find was of Rs. 149. What do we do now?"

"We'll buy it. I have the money."

As she was paying for it at the counter, I thought how she got the money. Mom never gives us any pocket money. She always gets us the things we want. It was then that it struck me. Didi had used up the money she was trying to save to buy that beautiful bracelet she had seen at the expensive jewellery shop at the mall. It was made on a silver chain and had little pink hearts hanging from it. I had caught her looking at it longingly many a times. It really was a pretty bracelet. When Didi had asked mom for it she had said that there was no use buying a bracelet made of silver as

Didi is well known for misplacing her things. I knew that Didi would never lose the bracelet if she ever got it. *She would value it more than her life.*

"Let's go Nitya . . . Hello! Where are you lost? God, you are so lost these days!" She began to flap her hands madly in front of my face.

"Wait, Didi! I am coming. Don't leave me here!"

CHAPTER-5

THE EMPTY PLATE

"Shhh . . . keep quiet. Don't make so much noise!" Didi and I were putting milk and biscuits out for Ginger. Didi had finally agreed to help me out on this mission, provided I gave her half of the cake when we make it. I was hoping we would be able to see her when she came.

After we had put down the plate we went behind the door curtains and waited. I was pretty excited to see her. Will she come? I had my doubts. She had come at three the other night. I wasn't ready to wait till then. Well, right now all we could do was wait. So that was what we did.

"How long will it take Didi?" I was growing more and more irritated by every passing second. Even though I knew she wouldn't arrive so early, I kept on bothering my sister, just for some sadistic pleasure.

"How am I supposed to know? I am sitting here with you, aren't I? You are so stupid!"

"Maybe she has seen us." I said. I pretended to not get offended by her calling me stupid. I pretended I hadn't even heard it.

"Oh yes! You're right. She won't come if we are sitting here. Let's go and sleep."

"Sleep!? But we did all this just to see her . . . then why are we sleeping?"

"You and I both are very sleepy right now. We will go to sleep today. And we will think of a better plan tomorrow. Meanwhile, the cat will get comfortable in this house."

***Elder Sibling Rule #51**: They are intelligent and vicious creatures. Don't underestimate them.*

"Oh. OK." I was agreeing to sleep but still thought that what we were doing was wrong. Why should we sleep? I was too sleepy to argue with her today. "We will discuss the matter later . . ."

"Come on, let's sleep. Grab your blanket, don't forget it. It is freezing cold today."

"*Yawn* . . ."

Oops . . . too loud . . .

"Too sleepy my dear? I thought you would be waiting all night for the cat?"

"Ugh! Leave me alone!" I pulled the blanket up to my face and closed my eyes. My sister was really annoying me today.

The next thing I knew, it was morning and the sun was shining through the window.

"Did she come?" I asked.

"I don't know." Didi said, carefully getting up and folding her blanket in a perfect fold. "Let's go and check."

Didi and I went to the kitchen to check up on our pet. Our *pretend* pet, Ginger.

I don't know why but I felt really excited when I was walking towards the kitchen. I was anticipating to see if she had really come. When both of us entered the kitchen, a familiar yet disappointing sight was waiting for us. Our maid, Shanti, had already started to do the dirty dishes from the night before!

All the dishes were being sprinkled with some hot, boiling water so that they get warm and do not freeze her hands when she washes them. The mornings in December get really cold, and so does the water.

"Shanti Didi, did you see a plate and a glass kept over there?" I said, pointing towards the counter where we had kept the plate full of biscuits and the glass full of milk.

"Which glass and plate are you talking about? There are so many of them here," she said, pointing towards the soap lathered utensils.

"Actually we wanted to see that . . ." Oh oh. What muddle have I gotten myself into? What do I say now? Wouldn't it look awkward if I say that I am putting all the food out for a cat? Our maid was very superstitious. She might even leave work if we tell her the truth. Cats are on the top of her *'Bad Omen'* list.

"Actually it was a fermentation science project." Wow! Didi to my rescue. This is one of the few times when my braniac Didi's brain helps. I never really understood how my Didi does it. She manages all her projects, gets highest marks in all her exams, goes to a dance class, tennis class and is a black belt in **taekwondo**[5]. Yet it seems to me that she never really studies. All she does all day is chat with her friends

---

[5] **Taekwondo:** A martial art originating in Korea. It combines combat and self-defense techniques with sport and exercise.

on the computer, talks to them on the phone and text messages them all day.

"Oh! You should have told me earlier. I have already rinsed all the utensils with water. Tell me how that plate looked like, I might recognize it."

"I don't quite remember myself. I was late for my project and thus did it when I was half asleep. By the way; was there any plate with biscuits in them, or any glass with some milk in it?" I pleaded.

"I don't understand what you mean. But there was no plate and glass which had something left in it. I always tell your mother when I see some plate that has food left. Now go, kids. I have a lot to do."

This information came like a relief to me. Didi and I exchanged quick smiling glances.

"What are you kids doing here? And what is the thing about milk I hear? Did any of you did not finish their milk? Now go and get ready for school, will you? Nitya, it's very good that you are able to score good marks but you have to finish your homework too. Which you did not do yesterday. Now go get ready fast and finish your homework. Neha, you go and start getting ready. You have thankfully finished all of your homework."

Wow! I wonder how she knows all of this. Does she sleepwalk in the night and check if I have done my homework or not? I couldn't do my homework as I was busy playing on my PSP and having coconut chocolates from the fridge, which we got as a gift.

"Ok, I'm going now. I don't have a lot of homework. I'll do it in less than 5 minutes." I lied. I had a lot of Science work to finish but if I tell her that, she will freak out and go ballistic on me. I didn't want any of that.

I did as I was told and got ready like a bolt and started doing my homework. It felt weird and out of place doing homework in the morning. I had done only about half of it when the time ran out and I had to rush off to the bus stop.

As I was walking to the bus stop, I thought I heard a cat's purr. Was that Ginger? I looked around me. A black cat with green eyes was staring back at me. She was sitting behind a flower pot, looking meek and purring away. I thought she looked hungry. Am I imagining things? I kept on looking for signs of her even when she was out of sight.

I kept on thinking about how much I want to see Ginger. I stared out of my bus onto the busy street. People were running, walking and some were even sleeping on the sidewalk. There seemed to be a million school buses going with seats packed with children of various schools. When I saw a news reporter shooting at some old shop; it struck me. A camera! I can keep it recording the whole night and finally get to see how she looked like. The more I thought about it, the more the plan began to shape beautifully in my mind.

CHAPTER-6

THE SELECTION TEST

By the time I reached school, I had it all decided. I would need a lot of Didi's help for this endeavor. I had already given her all my possessions to help me in other matters. I had nothing left to trade. I absentmindedly reached my classroom, put down my bag and sat down. Taking out my books for the first class, I felt happy. Nothing could ruin my good mood. On the other end of the classroom, Natasha was showing off her new pencil box. It was *obnoxiously* pink and had Barbies all over it. My pencil box, on the other hand, was plain black with only one zip. I had been using it since I had started school. I never really was the one who liked new things. I believed that everything would get old eventually so why bother wasting money? Even Natasha's new box would lose all its Barbie stickers and the glue would turn black. Even then, she will not realize the truth and buy another, only to have it turn out exactly the same way. Some people never change.

"Hey Nuts, show us your pencil box." Natasha sneered, bouncing all the way to my seat, breaking my train of thought. I am Natasha's punching bag, a thing I really don't mind being, as long as she doesn't do anything which affects my studies and my schoolwork. I hate people like Natasha with bubbly and sugar sweet voices, they seem so fake. Natasha is second on this list. You know who ranks **Numero Uno**[6] here. Hint, hint!

"I think you already are very content with your own *million dollar baby*, why do you want mine?" I used the name of an English Movie my sister was watching a couple of days ago. I was pretty sure Natasha didn't get the joke. Several girls sniggered. I knew I was mean, but there is only so much I can take.

"Well . . . don't be so rude. I was only asking." Her sugary voice had fused me.

"Don't!" I fumed.

I had spoken too fiercely. I regretted my words a minute after I had said them. The whole class was quiet and was staring at us now. I could feel Natasha

---

[6] **Numero Uno:** (In Spanish) means number one.

getting angrier by the second. I didn't want the fight to continue.

"I only wanted to ask if you wanted my old one now . . ."

I noticed how Natasha had changed her tone hastily. Her almost apology had now turned into a retort. I was pretty sure she didn't mean to say that. She just did it to make it up as I had embarrassed her. Natasha had always been the meaner one of the duo. Divya just sat and watched the fun. I've never found her saying anything. She even looked like the girl I might get along with as we share the same interests but due to her always staying with Natasha, I never had the guts. Today too, she was sitting and watching, never uttering a word.

"Okay students, I have good news for you." The teacher had entered at precisely the right moment. I was glad. I wanted to get out of the conversation with Natasha as soon as possible or as Didi would have said, '*ASAP*!'.

This made me sit up in my chair anyway. Good news! Could I have topped in another exam? But my last was 3 days ago and the teacher couldn't have possibly checked it by now. What could it be this time?

"Today we are conducting a small quiz that I mentioned a few days ago to select the top 4 children who will be representing our class in the 'MathsWhiz' competition. All those who wish to participate can go to the Examination Hall right now. The rest will go to the field and report to Verma Sir, The PE teacher. He will be conducting a small workshop on sports and some yoga. Ok? If you have any questions, you can ask me."

The Maths quiz! I had totally forgotten about that. I wanted to participate but I hadn't really prepared for it. I didn't want to give the exam now without preparing at all. I wanted to study first, now I had no chance. This dream of mine was crushed. There was no way I can prove myself worthy now. *Didi had won this one without even participating*. I looked around the classroom for any one who wanted to ask a question. Only one hand rose up. It was Rohit's. *Who else?*

"Excuse me Ma'am,"

"Yes Rohit, do you have a question?" Rohit was known to ask very peculiar questions. Most teachers did not even pick on him when he raised his hand in the class.

"It was written on the notice board that it was going to be an oral quiz. Why are we going to the examination hall?" It was common knowledge that the Examination Hall was used to conduct written examinations. It had strict looking chairs and tables and white walls. There were no pictures or posters on the walls. That room is scarier to me than the Principal's office. Not that I have been to the principal's office.

I wonder how the teacher will reply to this. I didn't have any problem with a written test too. After all, I had scored highest marks in English.

"Good question, Rohit. The test will be very easy. It will be multiple choice questions. All you have to do is tick mark the right choice. This is the easiest way to conduct the selection test. We couldn't possibly have an oral exam for everyone now, right?"

No one had any questions after this. I got up from my seat and silently started walking towards the Hall. It was on the other end of our school. Our school wasn't that big, but it wasn't small either. It was of the most perfect size. There were 3 buildings in our school and it was covered with lush green trees and colorful flowers. There was hardly any dirt around the school. We had a number of dustbins which everyone put trash in. Our school even had a tennis court, a basketball court and a football field. I looked inside the tennis court as I was walking. I saw Didi playing tennis. I sometimes envied her tennis playing ability. Her shots were so smooth yet so powerful. I play tennis too but not as tactfully as she does. One of her shots goes to the left edge of the court, the other goes on the right. I could see her opponent getting tired running all over the court. She noticed me staring at her and gave me a wink. I smiled back.

When I reached the Hall I grew a bit scared. There were so many children in there that I thought I had no chance. But there were supposed to be 4 kids from each section. We had 4 sections. That meant that 16 people had to be selected. I thought I might make it after all. I was practicing Mental Maths without even realizing it.

"Okay students. Take your seats. Each section will occupy one row. The exam is going to start soon."

I looked at the students from my section that had come for the test. There were those Maths toppers who could solve the 5th grade books. There was Rohit too. I saw 6 more people from my class.

I was pretty sure the two Maths toppers were going to get in. But I consoled myself by saying that there were still 2 places left. I *could* get in. I reminded myself to stay positive and focused.

The teacher distributed the question paper. I took deep breath and read the first question, then the second, the third . . . I couldn't believe my eyes. The paper looked so simple! All of these questions were framed in a tough way but I could see the hidden hint in all of them. I smiled. This was going to be fun. I took my pencil from my box and started solving the questions, smiling all the while.

I was one of the first ones to finish my paper. I looked around me. Everyone was still writing their exam. Did I leave some questions? I hastily rechecked my paper. It seemed fine. I looked over to see if the toppers had finished their paper or not. I was scared to see that they were still writing. Was the paper really that long? I looked harder; they appeared to be worried. It seemed like they couldn't answer the questions. They kept on murmuring and biting the ends of their pencils. Either I had got all the questions wrong or the paper really was hard for them. I couldn't believe it. They were both geniuses. They never got a Maths sum wrong. I am sure I was the one who messed up.

"Nitya! What are you up to?" the invigilator screamed. I was so surprised I jumped in my seat.

Oopsies, I shouldn't be peeking in someone's paper like that.

"5 minutes left, hurry up. I am coming to collect your answer sheets in a few minutes."

Everyone got in a state of panic. I wondered what was wrong. I went through my paper one last time. Again, I couldn't see any fault.

After the papers had been collected, the teacher announced that we were to go back to our classes. And that it was the last period. Wow! Time had flown by so fast. I must have missed cartloads of work.

I got back to my class to see my other classmates sweating and panting like they had just run a marathon race.

"How much work did I miss?" I asked Nainika. Nainika was a sweet girl who helps everyone.

"Work? No work at all." She fiddled with her shoelaces as she struggled to tie them. Her hands and shoes were muddy.

"None? But what did you do the whole day?"

"Oh! We were in the field. We had some workshops. Yoga workshops, races, that kind of thing."

"Oh! Seems like I haven't missed a lot of work then."

"Good Afternoon class!" I know it now. *Teachers are the reason for my lack of social life.*

"Today I will announce some exciting news. Remember the paragraph you had to write about your pet cat? I had not told you children but it was for an intraclass competition. I will be announcing the winners today. The winner will get an exciting prize."

Wow! Has our school started organizing all these contests lately? Or as they commonly say that I was *living under a rock*[7] and I didn't find out.

"There are going to be 3 winners," the teacher continued.

I know I stood no chance to win. Not that I want to win. English has never been my good subject anyway.

"The third prize goes to . . . Rohit! Well done. Your dog Roger seems very interesting."

We all clapped for him. Everyone knew he had a Golden Retriever named Roger. Roger's praises were heard by all in the class by Rohit day in and day out.

"Thank you Ma'am." Rohit said, beaming.

"The second prize winner is . . . Nainika. Everyone knows she does not have a pet. Those who didn't have one had to imagine. While everyone imagined normal pets like dogs, cats and hamsters, Nainika wrote about her pet dinosaur! Very imaginative! I like the part where you tried to turn him into a vegetarian . . . very funny!"

---

[7] **Living under a rock:** A common phrase used for someone who is oblivious and isn't up to date with the current happenings around them.

Wow! This was a very innovative idea. I tried to catch her attention and gave her a smile. She smiled back at me. Now those amazing entries had won the second and third prize, who won?

"The first prize winners' entry had a lot of spelling and grammatical mistakes. But I thought I should overlook them as this is a creative writing class, not a regular English class. The winner is . . . Nitya! Well done!"

It took me a second to realize that I had actually won. I got up from my seat and went up to the teacher's table. The teacher handed me a small packet packed with a red ribbon. Red was our school colour. Even our uniforms were a red skirt with a white shirt. I took the packet from the teacher's hands and went up to my seat. Everyone was smiling and looking at me. The only jealous glares were from Divya and Natasha. I don't know why they are the only ones who give me such jealous glances all the time. If they really want to win, why don't they try to do some work on their own sometimes?

"Okay class, settle down. Congratulations to all the winners. The ones, who didn't win, don't lose hope. There will be contests like these every month. But we won't tell you which one is a contest. So do your good in all of the exercises that we give you."

CHAPTER-7

SISTERLAND

The teacher started to write on the board. The next topic was,

"MY SISTER/BROTHER
(Can be younger or smaller. Assume if you don't have a sibling.)"

Everyone started to write thinking this is going to be a contest. I took the time and decided to look inside the packet that I had won. I undid the ribbon and looked inside. There seemed to be a lot of things inside. I saw some bookmarks, toffees, erasers shaped like Mickey Mouse and an envelope. I tore up the envelope. It had a gift voucher inside! It was a Rs. 250 voucher to Bookworld, an amazing bookstore at the mall. But to say the least I wasn't much of a bookworm. My sister was the biggest bookworm though. She would sit and read for hours. Thinking about it, Bookworld also has some amazing stationary. It has cute pencils, erasers, notebooks that I really like. Whenever we go to Bookworld Didi always goes gaga. She picks up a million *(sic)* books and keeps them on the counter, hoping she could buy all of them. During her gaga act mom and dad just look at her and exchange glances. I pity them. What have they got themselves into?

I started writing about her. This had given me an exciting topic to start writing about. Soon I was too engrossed in my work to notice . . .

MY SISTER
-Nitya Sharma

"Nitya, will you be faster! Come on, don't take so long!"

Didi was practically shouting on top of her lungs. We were going to a bookshop today as it was her Birthday. She doesn't like to have normal birthday parties like inviting her friends and chilling out at the mall. She makes the whole family go to the bookshop with her and buy books. How boring! After purchasing about a million books she finally decides that she is done for the day. Then we all have to go with her to a Chinese restaurant. I don't like Chinese restaurants. But of course, what I don't like automatically becomes her hobby . . .

"Nitya we are going and leaving you, okay? You have *roti-sabzi* in the house and I will go and have Chinese from Chinese-King restaurant. Have fun! See ya!"

She isn't so bad, actually. She is just a big fan of reading books. She helps me a lot in my homework as she knows a lot. Ask her anything and she will answer it in a second. She gets full marks in all her exams too. She might be like a dream sister for others, but sometimes she acts like a monster and I wish I could replace her. I'll narrate an incident which is a daily occurrence between us. If I am just sitting there, doing my work and out of curiosity, I open one of her books lying there on her bedside counter and flip open a page. I am then surrounded by sudden shrieks . . .

"Nitya! What do you think you are doing? You are not allowed to touch any of my books, understand? I am trying to keep them in *'mint'* condition! Mom, *MOM*! Tell her to get away from *my* stuff!"

Okay, chill out Didi. That's what I try to tell her amidst her shrieks. I am not intending on doing any harm. What does *'mint'*[8] condition mean anyway? Isn't *'mint'* a kind of candy flavour? And what has books got to do with it? And even though I promise her that I'll buy her more minty polos, she just won't understand.

But sometimes she can be super sweet. Like the time when I had forgotten to do my project and I wasn't feeling too well, she volunteered to do it for me.

She is very pretty with medium length brown hair that she ties up in a ponytail all the time, even when she is sleeping! She is tall and fair skinned.

---

[8] **Mint condition:** The term mint condition is often used to describe a collectible item such as an action figure, comic book, or toy that is as good as new without any scratches or other damage.

She is pretty strong, too. What else do you expect; she is a Black Belt in Taekwondo. She can just pick me up when I am troubling her and dump me on the bed. She runs away to mom by the time I wake up and overcome the shock. Till then she is too near to mom to try to attack again.

Elder Sibling Rule #49: *Mothers are their allies. Never attack them in front of mothers of any kind.*

Anyway, whatever she does, I still love her. I don't know whether she loves me or not. But we can always hope. But you know what they say about hope, it breeds eternal misery.

CHAPTER-8

SWEET AS CAKE

As soon as school ended I rushed home to tell my plan to Didi. I met her on the bus too but she was chatting away to glory with her friends so I thought I shouldn't bring up the matter in front of them. Didi's friends were always looking for excuses to pull my cheeks to which Didi replies *"Oh please . . ."*

"Didi," I said, excusing us from her gang of friends when we got out of the bus. "Can we reach home fast? I have an exciting plan. It's about Ginger. I have thought of a way that we can actually see her without actually having to stay awake at night."

"Oh, WOW!" *Sarcasm . . . the new teenager's greeting.*

"Come on Didi, fast please!"

"Okay, okay, chill I'm coming. The world isn't ending, you know. It has been postponed for 3013 now."

We reached home faster after this bit of conversation. But Didi had to speak to her friends till the last possible minute.

We finally reached home.

"Okay, now tell me the urgent news! You didn't let me speak to my friends!"

I took a deep breath and slowly tried to get the words out of my mouth.

"You know, we can't stay up all night. So I thought, why don't we use a camera?"

This caused Didi to sit up and notice. For a minute she was quiet. She just stared at me. Then slowly she began to understand what I meant. I think she was a little disappointed that she didn't come up with the idea first.

"That is just an amazing idea, dude!" *Dude*. This word gives me the creeps. What is it supposed to mean? *Dude*. It annoys me to no limits. But for now I had to cope up with it. I didn't want to change the topic. I wasn't ready for a lecture on the importance of the word *'Dude'* in the lives of obnoxious teenagers.

"Do you think you could fix the camera so that it stays on the whole night?"

"Yes. That won't be a problem."

"Cool! Thanks sis, you are the best."

"Don't call me 'sis,'" She gets so annoyed when I call her sis. But she never even pays a slightest bit of attention when I tell her I that I feel bad when she calls me 'lil'.

"Do you want to help me make the chocolate cake? We have to make it for mom, right?"

Elder Sister Rule #26: *When the mountain is about to explode, put it out with water. That means, when the object in question is about to go crazy with rage, change the topic. Preferably to something in which the object in question is good at. Start praising. In short, rouse the fire before it rises.*

"Yes! Let's go." The trick worked. She got all excited once again.

Thanks rule book, you saved my life.

We went to the kitchen and started to make the cake batter. We mixed all the ingredients that were needed—oil, water and eggs. We put the instant mix into it last. After all this was done we put it in the microwave and waited for it to bake. As we were sitting and waiting, I suddenly remembered about the happenings of the day.

"Didi, I won the English surprise essay competition."

"Oh wow! That's nice. What did you write about?"

Busted! "Nothing, just . . . umm . . . about the . . . ."

"What did you write, Nitya? Is it a rant about me?"

It *was* a rant about her. But that wasn't the topic that made me win.

"No. It's about . . . cats . . . Ginger."

Would she laugh? Or would she be angry? We can just wait.

"Um . . . you really are obsessed, aren't you? Did you get any prize?"

"Yes, some goodies." I showed her the goodies. When I reached to the voucher . . . Umm I can say she got very interested in *THAT*!

"I want it, want it, and want it! Please please please! Pretty pretty please with a cherry on top?"

Oh oh! I think I have to change the topic now.

"I also had the entrance test for the Maths quiz."

"For the what?"

I hate when she does that. She perfectly and clearly hears what I said but still she keeps on saying *what* as if she can't believe what I say.

"Maths quiz. I told you and mom the other day, didn't I? I had the entrance test for it today."

"How did it go?"

I started to tell her about it when the microwave went off. We rushed in to see how the cake had come out. It sure smelt heavenly! It looked heavenly too. It looked all soft and creamy and felt like it could melt in your mouth. We took it out and kept it on the table with the help of mittens. But a cake needs icing, right?

"What do we do for the icing?" I asked. Not sure if she would know anything that could help us out.

And guess what? She did.

"Do you still have the milk chocolates mom had got you?"

When mom gave us the money to buy the chocolates, she bought some herself too. She probably thought that Didi would keep the money and not buy me chocolates. Wow. Then why did she give us the money in the first place? Mother logic.

"Yes. I don't like them."

"Okay. That's awesome. Do you have the food colouring that you needed for a project once?"

"Yes, but why? It's in red colour. That's the only colour I have left."

"Okay! Awesome times two. Go to the fridge and get me all these things. Get the chocolate syrup we put in our milk too."

I went and got all that she needed—milk chocolates, red food colour and chocolate syrup. I still didn't understand what she possibly had to do with this.

She took some aluminum foil and made a cone. She left a little bit at the end through which she would ice the cake. She put in the chocolate syrup and began spreading. The uneven cake became smooth when she put the syrup. She covered the whole cake in it. She put the cake in the fridge. I looked on, confused as never before.

"What? You still didn't get it?"

"What will you do with the milk chocolates and the red colour?"

"Wait . . ." She said dramatically. "And watch!"

Elder Sibling Rule #80: *If she says something. Do it. Don't argue. They are worse than mothers when it comes to getting angry at not obeying their orders, however stupid and pointless they may be. Which, ninety percent of the time, they are.*

Well, if that's what she wants me to do, I'll do it. No problem.

She cut out little chunks of the white chocolate and melted them into a paste in the microwave. Then she mixed it with red colour to get a red coloured paste.

"Wow, Nice idea!"

"Cool, right? Now will you help me draw patterns on it?"

"Yup, of course!"

We both made a kind of swirly design on it. Then we covered it with little hearts. It didn't look very professional, but it sure looked pretty. Didi surprised me by putting coloured sugar confetti on it. The cake looked heavenly. I hoped it would taste as good as it looks.

"We're all done! Now put it in the fridge and we will wait for mom to come back home."

With this remark she went to her room, took out her latest book, the Hunger Games, and literally got lost in it. She gets so engrossed into her books that she forgets about the outside world. She doesn't move. She stays still, very still. Her eyes move back and forth, back and forth reading every line. Her hands move once in a while to turn over the page. She can sit like this for hours. I can't and I admit it. I will get so fidgety in 15 minutes. But Didi is so still that it's scary. I sometimes feel like Voldemort has petrified her. ***"Petrificus Totalus!"*** [9]

---

[9]   **Petrificus Totalus:** Used to temporarily bind the victim's body in a position much like that of a soldier at attention; this spell does not restrict breathing or seeing, and the victim will usually fall to the ground.

"Ding, dong . . . ."

Looks like mom's home. I looked over to see Didi. She was staring at her book as if she hadn't heard the bell. I sighed. Typical Neha behavior. I went over and opened the door. Both my parents were home. I welcomed them and offered water. Still no sign of Didi's awakening to the real world.

"Where's Neha?" Mom asked me. Papa on the other hand, started flicking through the news channels.

"Lost in her world. Again."

Mom looked at me and smiled. She seemed to be in a good mood. I thought I caught a twinkle in her eyes.

"So, anything special?"

I told her all about the essay competition and the Maths entrance test.

"That's very good. I'm proud of you!"

I went and secretly told Didi that mom and dad were home and we had to give them the cake. She got up. We put the cake neatly in a beautiful tray and went to their room. Mom was punching away to glory on her Blackberry and dad was engrossed in the news.

Mom saw us coming and got surprised seeing that big cake.

"Wow! Kids, did you two make that on your own? That's very good. Looks yummy!"

"We made that on our own mom. Really," Didi said. Looking very pleased at all the attention she was getting. Hello? I helped too . . .

We got plates, cut out big slices and offered it around to everyone. I bit into the cake with excitement. How would it taste? It tasted awesome! It was gooey and seemed to melt in your mouth. I finished mine before everyone and asked mom for more.

"It's really a wonderful cake. I can't believe you both could do something together. It's a mystery!" Papa joked.

"Do we really fight a lot?" I asked. We fight, but not that much that we can't even do anything together.

"Yeah, do we?" Didi chimed in.

"Whatever you do, you both still are my little princesses."

We both went and gave dad a hug. He presented us with a 100 rupee note each to spend in the school canteen. I never get money to spend in the canteen while all our friends get money almost everyday. Somehow that made it very special for me.

We went out for dinner that day. We visited this new restaurant that opened up nearby called *"Around the World"*. It had food from various cuisines. That meant that Didi and I won't fight for the restaurant. Mom and dad ordered Indian Thali. We have Indian food in the house everyday! Shouldn't we try something special when we dine out? Anyways, I tasted a bite. Somehow it tasted different from the one we have at home. It was yummy. Why can't she make dinner like this every day? I would eat it without a problem. I would even ask for second helpings of everything.

Didi as usual ordered Chinese food. No matter how much in good terms I will be with Didi, I would never try out Chinese food. But I decided to break my pact today. Who knew, maybe Chinese food will suit my taste buds now that I am a professional chocolate cake baker? The vegetables didn't look inviting to me at all. Anyways, I tasted it. I thought it would taste like noodles, but all I could taste was carrots, capsicums and all of these veggies mixed in vinegar. I figured out I would be better off without trying the food. My taste had been spoiled. I dank water to wash the sick taste down my throat. Didi laughed.

Elder Sibling Rule #43: *They are sadistic creatures. They set fires to feel joy.*

We returned home late. As I was about to go to sleep when Didi's *Iphone* beeped.

"Didi, you aren't allowed to use your phone after 10 at night. Who is this? What if I tell mom?" I said, mockingly.

Didi looked panicked; obviously she was scared that mom would see her. She looked around the room and picked up her phone. Then, hearing what I had said, mouthed the words *'shut up'* at me. I didn't mind. I had grown accustomed to it. She stared at the phone for a long time and said, "You forgot! Ginger. I had put the timer in my phone."

"Oh no! What do we do now? Could you please put the camera on? I hope it's not too late."

Didi thought for a while.

"Okay. Let me get it first. You go put the biscuits and milk."

I did as I was told. She put the camera on and adjusted it towards the window. After all this was done, we went to sleep. Boy, was I exhausted!

CHAPTER-9

A Failed Plan

The next morning I woke up on feeling something cold being sprinkled on me and saw that Didi was already awake. A huge wave of nostalgia hit me. She was waking me up by sprinkling water on my face. I didn't want that on a cold December morning!

"Come on, we have to see what Ginger is up to. Chill, mom and dad are not awake yet."

I was very sleepy yet I got out of my bed and followed her towards the kitchen.

The food and the milk were gone! That meant that Ginger had come. I headed towards the camera to see what it had caught. The camera was off. I looked towards Didi. Had she forgotten to turn it on?

"Didi, why is the camera off? Had you forgotten to turn it on last night?" My sister is very systematic. I knew she wouldn't have forgotten something as important as turning it on.

Didi looked at me, surprised. She grabbed the camera from me and checked its settings.

"No! I had turned it on. I remember too clearly. But the camera only had a 3 hour recording memory left and it shut down midway! I doubt if it saved the video or deleted it."

"Oh no!"

"Our plan has failed, lil sis."

I thought for a moment. Then smiled.

"What are you smiling at? Don't you get what this means? You are so naïve!"

"What if she came during the three hours the camera was recording? We would have caught her then."

Didi looked at me. I sure watched a lot of cartoons, but it paid off eventually.

"That's an amazing idea! We will need to charge the camera first. Now let's go to school. I'll put it on charge right now and by the time we return back it will be fully charged. We'll see the clips when we return and mom won't be home."

Elder Sibling Rule #2: *They are more 'experienced' than you are.*

"Okay. Let's go."

That whole day at school I was super excited. I wasn't paying any attention to what the teachers were saying and got scolded quite a few times.

During Maths class I realized that I had spent half my time staring at the picture of the cat and kitten in the *"Animals and their young ones"* poster in our classroom!

"Nitya! I know cats are interesting but I think *division* is a lot more important! Pay attention!"

"Sorry Ma'am." I didn't even look at the poster the whole period. That took a lot of will power, if I say so myself.

Towards the end of the day I knew that if I continued to behave like this, teachers would tell my mom about my absurd behavior and my mom would freak out. So I started to try and pay attention in class.

As soon as the bus stopped, I rushed off to my house and turned on the lights. No one was at home. Mom and dad were both in their respective offices. Our maid would come at around three to do the dishes. I looked in the fridge while I was waiting for Didi to stop blabbering to her friends and come home. Mom always leaves us some food in the fridge which Didi microwaves and gives us for lunch. Today, there was rajma and rice. I liked rajma and rice and so did Didi. Well, she liked to eat everything and anything that is edible and in her sight. I wonder how she remains so thin. Maybe because she does so many sports and exercises. I, on the other hand, just don't like to eat a lot of food. Mom says I eat like a bird. Didi, being a lot more scientific in her insults, says I am a picky eater.

At last after what seemed like hours, Didi finally entered the house looking tired and flushed. She had a tennis match with a neighboring school today. That was the reason she was still in a tennis skirt and shirt, with a jacket draped on her. It was December yet she was wearing a skirt and half sleeved top. No wonder she was shivering. The moment she came inside the house she went to her room and changed. I didn't blame her. I would've done the same. After all, your health was more important than the video of a cat. She came back a few minutes later, wearing track pants and a sweater. She had stopped shivering now and had mom's shawl draped on her. During normal days I would have teased her saying that she looked like an aunty. But I had stopped teasing her nowadays after I found out how sweet she could be when she wanted to. I wanted her to stay that way.

"Didi . . ." I decided I would bring the matter up slowly. It looked like she had forgotten all about it.

"Yeah?" She sounded irritated.

"Umm . . . How was your match today? Did you win?" I hastily changed my question.

"Yes, I did win. It was a hard match. We both were playing neck to neck."

Elder Sibling Rule #97: *They always win at whatever they do. If they don't, they blame it on you. Beware!*

Why did I even ask? She had won, of course.

"That's very cool. When are you treating your coach, **A.K.A.**[10] me?" I joked. I had to make her mood lighter.

"Ha-ha, very funny, *coach*. BTW, what's for lunch?"

Sigh . . . Didi and her lingos . . .

"BTW? Isn't that some kind of a car?" I didn't understand anything she was saying. I never did.

---

[10]   **A.K.A. :**Also known as

"BTW! It means *By The Way*! Didn't you know that? And BTW is not some kind of a car. That's BMW. Got it, Dumbo?"

"Oh! Now I get it. *BTW,* there is rajma—rice for lunch." I hand—quoted BTW.

"Cool. Now go change and freshen up. Meanwhile I'll heat up the food."

I did as I was told. While we were eating our food Didi was constantly texting on her phone and talking to people. I was getting nothing but bored. We were sitting on our dining table. We aren't allowed to text or watch TV while eating at the dining table. But if Didi was breaking the rules and texting, I decided to open the TV. I reached for the remote and started to flick through the channels. I stopped where there was a cartoon showing. I loved *Chota Bheem*. I was watching it merrily when Didi stopped talking and texting on her phone. She reached for the remote in my hands.

"Hey! Not fair. I was watching." I said. Didi paid no heed to what I was saying.

"But I have to watch **'The Big Bang Theory'**[11]. Why don't you watch it with me? Let's watch something we both *enjoy*." She replied, putting emphasis on 'enjoy'.

---

[11]   **The Big Bang Theory:** A television series.

"But I want to watch a cartoon!" I was whining now.

"You want to watch a cartoon? Go look in the mirror. Leave me alone."

I really wished I would have called her aunty when I got the chance. I was so stupid when I thought Didi was sweet.

"Ha-ha, very funny. I am not a cartoon. You are."

I fidgeted around. I wanted to tell her that I wanted to see the camera. She sensed it right away.

"What is happening to you? Is there something you want to tell me?"

Mind Reading Device is working perfectly fine . . .

I decided to break the ice.

"Put the camera on. I want to see if Ginger came last night."

"Oh! I totally forgot. So that's what you wanted to tell me all along? Why didn't you say so earlier?" I wanted to tell her I was scared of her. I didn't say so.

"Let's go watch it!"

We went to mom's room and opened the drawer where the camera was kept. Didi fiddled with it for a while and said, "Let's go attach it to the TV. Then we both will be able to see it clearer than the small screen of the camera."

I sometimes envy Didi's mind. I really do.

"Ok."

She took out our TV's set-top-box cord and replaced the wires with the ones on the camera. Then she put on the TV and clicked on the power button. Suddenly, what the camera was shooting came on the TV. This way we could see what we were shooting. Didi put on last nights video and pressed play.

But lo and behold! All we could see was pitch black screen and we could hear faint hooting of the owls and the bats. Without the light on in the kitchen, we couldn't see anything! We could faintly make out the window though. Didi and I exchanged glances. This wasn't as we had thought it would be.

"Oh no!" Didi said. "Now what do we do?"

I looked at her disappointed face. I couldn't help hiding mine too.

"There has to be a way . . ." I said. After all, we had to keep our hopes up.

We both knew mom would come and switch off the light at night if we kept it on.

Didi, meanwhile, kept on fiddling with the knobs and buttons of the camera. Then she shouted,

"Eureka! I got it! The night settings on our camera!"

"What? I didn't get you." I said, trying to make sense of what she had just said.

"Our camera has a night setting which enables us to take brilliant footage with extremely low light! We could also lower the pixels in our camera and empty the memory stick to take the video of the whole night! Why didn't I think of that before?"

I looked at her, bewildered and shocked. Sensing the shock Didi slowly said, "I know you didn't understand a word of what I am saying, but relax. I've got it all figured out."

Just this once, I decided to trust her.

"Okay." I said, dejected.

"Now go and do your homework."

We finished eating our food and went to our rooms to finish our homework. I didn't have any because of the entrance tests but I took out one of my extra books to study for the MathsWhiz Olympiad. But I didn't even know that I was selected or not. I was so bored I did it anyway. After studying for atleast 2 hours I decided to go watch some TV. But Didi had, like always, taken hold of it. She was watching some English movie. Why does she watch those anyway? I don't understand the way they speak English. It doesn't even seem like

English to me. But Didi seems to understand it very well and even sings along to its songs. I don't find this unusual though, English has never been one of my strong subjects.

CHAPTER-10

A THRILL

That night I was sure I was going to be able to finally see Ginger. I waited excitedly as Didi adjusted the camera between some containers of salt and sugar. We had tested out the night vision settings earlier that day and it had worked brilliantly. We also adjusted a small torch towards the window just in case the night setting do not work well enough. We covered the mouth of the torch with some butter paper so as to dim the glow a bit. This was, obviously, Didi's idea. I was super excited.

I fidgeted in my bed but couldn't fall asleep for a long time. In the end Didi got irritated and started shouting at me.

"Stop it! Can't you go to sleep?"

"Okay, sorry." I replied but still I couldn't sleep. Didi was fast asleep in minutes though.

"Thump"

"Thump"

Was I dreaming? Or was Ginger finally here?

It was a faint noise coming from the street below us. We lived on the first floor and there were 3 floors in our building. I sometimes wished we had a lift in our building. Some of my friends' houses had lifts. Wouldn't that be so cool? I had asked Didi about that once. She said that our building doesn't have many floors and it doesn't need a lift. I am afraid she was right though, some of my friends who had lifts had buildings with up to 20 floors! Imagine the view from that high up. Our building has 3 floors, right? Even malls have three floors. Then why do they have lifts? And that too, multiple lifts? All this was way too confusing for me. I decided to let it go.

I looked all around my room, bored. I wasn't sleepy at all. I tried closing my eyes and tried to concentrate but I wouldn't doze off. How does a person *will* themselves to sleep anyway? I looked at my sister's bedside counter. It was neatly arranged and had a clock, a pen, a notepad and her latest book with a bookmark stuck in it. I took the book from the counter, anxious not to wake Didi up or she'll fight about her mint polos again. The book was very thick. I looked at the number of pages it had, and was surprised! It had over 300 pages! How could she read that many pages was beyond me. I read the title; it said *Harry Potter and the Half-Blood Prince*. I couldn't make any sense out of the title; I wonder how she could read the whole book. I put the book back in its place just as it was and picked up the notepad.

Didi is the most organized person I have met. She may even be the most organized person in the world. She never forgets anything and has all her homework done on time. She keeps 3 Planner diaries and maintains them regularly. One of them is for her personal list, one for her school list and one for her chore list. Then she even has a journal in which she writes down important information like test syllabi, project topics, etc. To top it all, she also has a business diary which she uses to write down everything she has to do each day. If she has a dance class due on 10th of December, she will write down, 'Dance class, 4 pm.' on the 10th December page. Wow! I can't even manage 1 dairy, let alone that many. I looked at her notepad. It had personal wishes in it. Her handwriting is surely something I could steal from her if I could. She has the most beautiful cursive writing. Even when she is in a hurry, her handwriting looks perfect. I know that I'm not supposed to see her diary but I can't help it. *Would you have seen it if you had a chance?*

I went through her list. It had pretty random wishes. I don't even have a list of these kinds of things, I just memorize them. But I do forget half the things I have to do. I guess Didi's planner isn't such a bad idea after all. But I knew I won't be able to manage such a diary, even if I try my level best.

After reading or examining all that was there in my room, I still couldn't sleep. I had once read that if a person can't sleep, they should count sheep. Maybe I should do that. Why do we count sheep anyway? Why not goats? Or cars? I guess it's your own choice. I would prefer to count *cats* instead. I pictured cats jumping over a fence made up of fifth grade Maths books.

"1,2,3,4,5 . . . 50,51,52 . . . 345,346,347 . . ."

This counting sheep thing doesn't work. Till where are you supposed to count anyway? Till a thousand? A lakh? A crore? I reached 500 but I didn't fall asleep.

"Thump"

What was that? Ginger? Woohoo!

I pinched myself to make sure I wasn't dreaming. I surely wasn't as my hand hurt.

"Thump"

"Thump"

I was so excited! Maybe today I will be able to see her.

"Meow, meow . . ."

It's surely a cat! It's Ginger! I couldn't believe it!

I got up from the bed, shivering as I had no socks on. I walked towards the kitchen with my feet freezing beneath me on the cold floor. I was walking merrily and didn't notice the pencil that was innocently lying on the living room floor. I accidentally stepped on it and lost my balance.

"Aaah!"

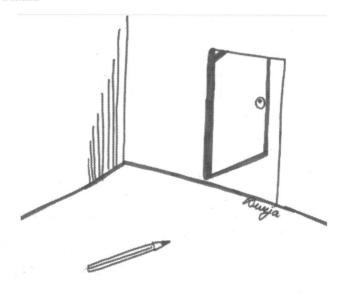

I screamed. I put out my hands out to balance the fall. I fell flat on my face. I never knew a pencil could make you fall like this. But it was too late, my fall had startled Ginger. She gave a departing meow and left. I rushed towards the kitchen on all fours as fast as I could because standing up would waste a lot of time. I couldn't see Ginger anywhere. But I did catch a slight glimpse of her tail just as she was leaving. I couldn't make out the color or the pattern on the tail, but it was a tail all right! I looked at the camera; it was still blinking a red light, indicating that it was recording. Tomorrow, no matter what, I would be able to see what Ginger looked like, and my quest would be over.

I went back to my bed. Before I knew it, I was fast asleep.

CHAPTER-11

ANOTHER DISAPPOINTMENT

"Wake up . . ."

"Come on, don't sleep that much!"

I was awakened the next morning by the shouts of Didi at 6:30 in the morning. We usually don't wake up before 7:00 as we live quite near to our school which doesn't start till 8.

"What is it?" I was groggy and sleep deprived. I don't even remember how long I had stayed up last night.

"You want to see Ginger or not?"

This sentence made me sit up in bed. Did I dream last night or had Ginger really come? I knew that if we saw the clips I would come to know if I had been dreaming or not.

"Yes! Let's go!" I practically shouted.

"Shhh . . ." Didi whispered, "You'll wake mom up."

"Oops . . . sorry." I whispered, looking around for signs of mom waking up.

We quietly got out of our beds and walked towards the kitchen. The house looked so scary, all empty and dark. I held on tight to Didi's hands. I wasn't afraid to admit that I was scared. We made our way towards the kitchen and quietly took the camera out from where we had kept it. We saw that the flashlight was not in its original position. Had someone come in there last night? We both must have been thinking the same things as Didi and I exchanged glances. I knew it wasn't me as I hadn't even come fully inside the kitchen and I was on all fours. It surely wasn't me.

"Didi, I don't think we kept the flashlight that way . . ."

"I know. It seems awkward. Anyway, come to the room, we'll see the movie on our laptop."

This was the first time Didi had said "our" laptop. Usually it's like, "Don't touch my laptop!" or, "Keep away from my laptop!" I have to admit, it felt good to see change. I hope it stays that way forever.

It took us 5 whole minutes to transfer the 7 hour video to Didi's laptop. After we had transferred it, we held our breath and pressed play. I felt like I was spying on someone. Nitya 007!

The video came up. I recognized our kitchen in a jiffy. The white drawers, the stove, the non-stick cookware and the familiar window; all of them looked just like they should. The lighting worked brilliantly and I could see everything clearly, even in the dark. As Didi was fast forwarding the video, we saw someone come in. Didi paused and rewinded the video. It was mom. We waited with our breaths held. Will we get caught? She had come in to take something. She was moving some containers around. We checked and calculated the time; it must've been around 2 when she came. Thankfully, she didn't come to know about the camera. As she was moving things around, one of the containers she moved hit the flashlight and it moved a little from its position. Thankfully mom didn't notice the flashlight due to its dim lighting. It swiveled like a top across the kitchen counter causing the kitchen to light up like a disco. But mom was too busy to notice. From the look of it, she had come to make some tea. The flashlight stopped moving eventually, just in front of our camera!

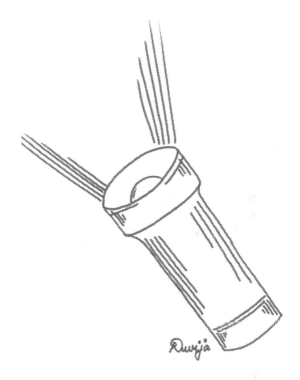

We held our breath. It was like watching a movie. The only difference was that you don't have to keep on looking at the door for mom's signs while watching a movie. I didn't know which mom to be more worried about, the one in the camera or the one who could wake up any instant. But it was exciting all the same.

The glare from the flashlight landed straight on our camera. And then we could see nothing else but the glare of the torch. It was just like the very first time we had put the camera, instead of being pitch black like it was last time, it was brilliant white. We fast forwarded it till we reached the end where we pick up the flashlight and camera and turn it off. What a disappointing video!

"Oh no . . ." I couldn't keep it in any longer. Our search has been jinxed.

"Our search has only brought us bad luck so far . . ."

We closed the laptop and put it back in its place. Mom was really finicky about keeping things in place. We both knew very well that if we don't keep the laptop back in its place on time, it could be confiscated. She would surely get to know we had used it way past our bedtime. I sometimes think our mom likes to confiscate our laptop. She is always looking for new things we do that may allow her to take our laptop away from us. Why did she get us laptops of she takes them back? *I feel like all mothers love confiscating things.*

As soon as we were done, we curled back in our beds and pretended to sleep. We heard mom coming to wake us up moments later. Phew! We were just in time.

"Wake up, time to rise and shine!"

She always tries to be cheerful while waking us up.

"Surprise!" We both yelled at the same time and we hadn't even planned it. This was the first thing that proved that we were sisters in about a decade of us living together.

"Oh you both are already up! What is the matter? Let the cat out of the bag!"

I told you she tried to act cheerful while waking us up.

"Nothing mom . . . Do we only do good things if we want something from you?" I asked. We couldn't be that bad, could we?

"No . . ."

Sigh. Mom continued to speak.

"Whenever you want something, you don't take the pain of doing something good, you just ask and crib untill you're done!" Mom was joking with us.

We got up from our beds and started to get ready for school. We both got ready 15 minutes earlier than usual. Didi decided to use this time to read her book.

We both were extra fresh and excited for school today. I had to get my results for the Maths Olympiad which I had totally forgotten about. I was forgetting things a lot these days due to being preoccupied with Ginger. She really took away most of my time. I hope I get in though. Hope is the only thing I could do right now as I hadn't prepared a bit for it.

CHAPTER-12

An Incorrect Accusation

"And the last person to be selected to represent our class in the Olympiad is . . ."

I held my breath and waited. Three names had already been taken. I wasn't selected yet. There were those two class toppers who finally made it in, and then there was Rohit. Only 2 other students in my class had participated. That meant I had 1/3 chance of getting in. I wanted to get in this so desperately that I absent-mindedly started applying Maths everywhere.

"Nitya Kumar! You got the highest score in our class. Well done. Seems like you are on a roll, first the English test, and now this. Has your sister been tutoring you?"

For a second I thought I was dreaming. But I stood up as the class applauded for the 4 children who were going to be representing the class. I looked at all the children. They were all clapping but they had mixed reactions. Divya and Natasha were giving me jealous and "I don't care" looks. This made it seem like they cared even more. They were clapping like they were swatting flies. Nainika was genuinely happy, or so it seemed. The other children were clapping too but I got a shock when I looked at the two Maths toppers. They were giving me angry looks! Why were they angry? Was it because I had gotten more marks than they had? It wasn't my fault, now, was it? I waited till recess to figure that out.

During recess I normally eat alone or sometimes with Nainika. The other girls are always crowding around Divya and Natasha. They both seem to have amazing lunch boxes. Pizzas, burgers, noodles, cakes . . . there was never a dull day in their lunch. But today even Nainika was with them. I went towards the two Maths toppers, who were engaged in an intense game of tic-tac-toe.

"Hello, guys!" I wanted to act cheerful. They were my new teammates, right? I *had* to be friends with them.

"Hi and bye." One of the boys replied. His voice was cold with no expression in his voice.

I decided to pretend I didn't hear that remark.

"Congratulations for making it to the team. Hope we win." I replied cheerfully.

"That's not possible at all now because now *you* are in the team with us."

"Well, that's harsh . . . and why won't you win when I'm there?" I demanded. They were getting on my nerves. I told myself to stay calm.

"Because you are a girl."

Wow! He sounded so casual when he said that. Like he called on girls like this every day and it was no big deal to him.

"And you are a boy. So what? It doesn't matter if you are a boy or a girl. It depends on whether you knew your stuff or not. It depends on how much you know. And I studied and I knew my stuff. So did you."

"Yeah, whatever . . . ever thought of becoming a teacher? You sound exactly like one."

This remark was too much for me. I had tried to stay calm for so long. But I could see it wasn't working . . .

"For your kind information, I was the one who scored the highest marks. Higher than both of you." I was practically shouting at them. I looked around to see if there was any teacher around. There wasn't. Everyone was crowding around Natasha's table as she was giving out free Belgian chocolates to everyone. I sighed. "How do you reckon I got in then?"

"You cheated. *Cheater*."

What? When did I cheat? I don't cheat. I am way too scared that I'll get caught. And cheating is a bad thing. I would never cheat. What are they saying?

"What are you saying? I never cheat. You are just accusing me. You're just jealous," I remarked.

"You cheated from our paper. I saw you. The teacher did too."

Oh! Now I remember. I wasn't cheating; I had finished my paper early and was looking around. But I wasn't sure what I would say to them. It doesn't seem like a good reason, they would never believe it.

"Okay, make accusations. See if I care. I can see it on your faces that you are jealous of the fact that I am a girl and made a higher score. Go ahead, accuse all you want. Also, just to let you know, if I had cheated from your paper, I would have scored equal or lesser to yours, not higher. Use your brains."

With this I walked away. I took my lunch box and went out to the field. It felt so good, out in the open. The wind was chilly. I had my coat on, so only my face felt cold. The icy cold wind began to sting my face, but I didn't care at all, I was numb from it all.

As I was walking, I saw Didi. She was with her friends, chatting away to glory. I decided to go talk to her as I had nothing else to do. I wanted to talk to *someone*.

"Didi, hi!" I said, trying to be cheerful. Inside, I wanted to cry.

"Hey, Nitya. What's up?"

Didi looked like she wasn't enjoying any bit of this conversation. Her face was sour. It looked like she didn't want me here.

"Actually I have nothing else to do. Can I eat my food with you?"

"Umm . . . No . . . I don't think so . . . I have Chemistry in a few minutes . . ."

Before she could complete her sentence, a friend of hers who I've never seen before started to pull my cheeks and it hurt. She seemed to be enjoying herself.

"Neha! Your sister is such a cutie pie . . ."

I beamed. It felt good to be called cute.

"Yeah, I know she is cute . . . hey Nitya, look, your friend is calling you." Didi said, pointing to the building where my classroom is.

I looked at the place she was pointing to. Who could it be? Did someone realize I hadn't cheated and come to say sorry? Had the toppers told the teacher and she had come to tell me that I wasn't in the team anymore? There were a lot of people there, but none of them was calling me. I didn't even recognize anyone.

"Where? I can't see anyone . . ." I said, puzzled.

"Come on, I'll show you." Didi took my hand and pulled me aside. She was holding my hand so tight that it hurt. Her hands were freezing cold.

"Leave me alone!" She hissed, her mouth shut tightly all the time. She turned back, smiled lightly at her friends and then turned to me again.

"But . . . w what did I I d do?" I stammered. I was scared. Did I do something wrong? Trust me, Didi's grip felt like hot, branding iron.

"Leave me alone, okay? I don't want to eat my food with *you*. I handle you at home already and you get on my nerves. I want you to leave me alone at least when I am in school. Now go."

Elder Sibling Rule #75: They are embarrassed by you in public. Never talk to them when they are with somebody else.

She was so harsh to me that I thought it would be better if I don't argue. I went towards my own classroom, disappointed. After everyone had turned their back at me, I felt I deserved a little sympathy from my own sister. What happened to her all of a sudden? She was alright when we were watching the footage in the morning. I walked towards the classroom, clutching my hand. Her hand had delved deep into my skin, and her nails created an impression. I wished she would have caught me by my arm, atleast my coat would have saved me.

"Trriiing."

Wow. Perfect timing. I reached my class and took my seat at the very back of the class. As I sat, I saw everyone staring at me. I looked at Nainika; she wasn't smiling as she usually is. She was glaring at me as if to say, "*I didn't expect this from you.*"

What had I done? The whole day I was ignored and even tripped by Natasha. She put her foot out as I was passing, and I fell on my face. I was then faced by the laughs of all the children around me. I felt embarrassed. I wanted to go home. I truly felt like I wanted the ground to open up and swallow me inside.

As soon as the final bell rang I leapt out of my seat and started to get out of my class. I didn't want to linger around for a second more. I knew that the tears would be bursting out any moment now and I wanted to be out of class before that happened.

I hastily began to walk out of the class, blinking back tears. As I was walking, I saw Natasha walking right behind me. I shifted to the side and let her pass. She passed by me and didn't even say a word of thanks. All I heard was a faint comment which knocked out the breath in mine, "*Cheater*". Several people heard it and whirled around to look at me. I felt embarrassed to be standing there and glared by 20 strangers whom I didn't even know. I joined two and two together and figured it out. The class toppers must have spread it out. And Divya and Natasha are always looking out for a reason to bring me down.

I wanted to get back to my home as fast as I could. I felt as if there was no one in the world who loved me anymore. Not even my own sister. My parents would obviously choose my sister over me any day.

I went to my room and lay down on my bed. I hadn't even changed out of my uniform. Didi called me for food, but I wasn't hungry. Before I knew it, I was fast asleep.

CHAPTER-13

A Dull Night

I woke up, and found out that it was 7 at night. I heard Didi in the other room, chatting on the phone. That indicated that mom wasn't home yet. Usually mom is home by 6:30. Either she has gone out again, or she is getting late. I looked at Didi. She seemed to have forgotten how she broke my heart at school today. Forgive and forget, taken too literally.

But I decided to ignore it too. I mean, I have friend problems at school, maybe she has too. I decided to let her deal with her problems, while I figured out how to deal with my own *incorrect accusation*.

I got up and went towards the room where Didi was chatting. I didn't want her to notice me; I had only gone in there to get my school bag which I had angrily dumped before dozing off. She seemed to notice me right away. She covered the phone with her hands and said, "Mom is stuck in traffic as it was raining. She will get back late. She told me to convey this message to you. Enjoy your freedom."

Saying this, she went back to her phone. I sighed. It felt great when mom wasn't home, but right now I wanted her here. I went and changed out of my school uniform, which I still had on. I then decided to do my homework. I didn't want to miss it again. I went towards the table, made a big deal of getting out all my books, anxious to make this as long as possible and mom to get back home soon. I wanted to hug her and feel like it was alright again. She would always give me strength when I needed it. I would tell her to make me hot chocolate then, hers is the best I've ever tasted. But I knew I'll have to while away my time till then.

"Nitya . . . Can I borrow your ruler?" Didi said, peeking from the curtain from her own table. I hadn't noticed her keeping down the phone and coming to study. Even though we share a same bedroom, mom says it is morally impossible for us to share a same room while studying. That's the reason why we had a curtain in between our study tables.

"Um, yes." I said, handing the ruler to her. She seemed to have forgotten.

Elder Sibling Rule #05: *If they mess with you, they'll forget it in a minute, but if you mess with them . . . God save you.*

Even though I didn't have a lot of homework, I tried to make the two Maths assignments to stretch as long as possible. But I knew they would finish sometime, and that they did.

"Do you have a sharpener?" Didi seemed to be on an asking spree today. I couldn't believe she could be mean and forget about it in a jiffy.

"Umm Didi . . . why don't you take my whole box? That ways you can use all you want and you won't even disturb me." I replied, adding just a hint of sarcasm into my voice.

"Yup . . . that'd be great!" Even more sarcasm. Her sarcasm was sweet, not sour.

I handed her the pencil box. Then I got back to my work.

A minute later she returned back my things and went inside the kitchen. She came back a minute later, carrying some hot chocolate and the cake we had made a few days ago.

"Is this for me?" I asked, as she put the plate down on my table.

"Yes, of course. I knew you hadn't eaten any lunch and thought you would be hungry. Why? You don't want it?"

"No . . . I mean yes. Thanks." I started eating my cake. The hot chocolate warmed me up thoroughly.

"By the way, sorry for the recess incident. I shouldn't have been so mean to you."

"It's ok. I shouldn't have interfered with your personal time too."

We hugged. I was happy Didi had said sorry.

That night was a quiet one. We ate dinner in silence as mom and dad both were very tired due to driving in the traffic. I was embarrassed as I didn't even get to know that it rained as I was sleeping. I hoped everyone would have forgotten about the *cheating* story by tomorrow.

CHAPTER-14

FINALLY WE MEET

"This time, the torch will be fixed by tape." Didi whispered to me after we had finished our dinner.

During the whole incidents of the day, I had forgotten about Ginger. We had tried everything, and everything had backfired. Our last try was foolproof. Nothing could go wrong.

"Okay."

We both were in the kitchen, fixing the camera again. Didi and I had made a pact that this was our last try and we would never try again if this didn't work. I had to admit I was getting a little bored and annoyed due to these constant failures.

Didi looked super sleepy. I wasn't sleepy, though. I was wide awake. This was due to the fact that I had slept a few hours in the afternoon but Didi hadn't. We hadn't been getting much sleep in the last few days due to Ginger.

"We're done!" Didi seemed to be really happy that we were all fixed. She was so sleepy that I bet she wouldn't have even done this if I hadn't bribed her. But I know a bit of blackmailing myself, staying with Didi all these years.

I went back to my room. Didi was so sleepy that she was asleep in no time at all. Only I kept awake. I was awake for a long time.

"Thump."

Oh my god! She was here! But I shouldn't call her a *she* yet. I wasn't completely sure of her gender. But then, do cats even have a gender? It seemed more logical to call her a she. I wanted her to be a she.

"Thump"

I had a small battle with myself, thinking if I should go or not. I finally decided to go. What if the flashlight or the camera is set wrong? I would never be able to see her that way. We had made a pact to not try this again. I got up. I realized that I didn't have any socks on. I somehow never have socks on when Ginger is about to come. Is it a co-incidence, or what? The floor was freezing. I quickly snuggled into my slippers and made my way towards the kitchen. There were no obstacles today. No pencils were lying on the floor. The camera was on, the flashlight fixed. This was it.

The kitchen looked so haunting without the lights on and the faint smell of food not coming from it.

"Thump . . . Meow . . ."

I looked in. Again, two pairs of mysterious black eyes greeted me. I willed myself not to faint. But I wasn't scared of them now. We both seemed to be thinking the same thing, as we both were standing there, staring at each other. I tried to put on my sweetest face, trying to tell the cat that I was a friend. She seemed to understand that. She stopped purring, and looked at me. I looked back, anxious not to say or do anything that might make her run away.

"Meow . . ."

She seemed to be the one to break the awkward silence. But her purr was not threatening; it was scared, and nervous.

I looked on. A part of me wanted to go out and pet her soft black fur, but a part of me was scared she might disappear, like a mirage in a desert.

I realized that she was a black cat, without a hint of Ginger in her. I felt awkward calling her Ginger.

We both were there, looking at each other, till what seemed like eternity. Finally I decided to make a start; after all, I was getting a bit bored.

"Hi, Gin—Kitty . . ." I said. I felt dumb but I waited for her reaction, anyway. She looked on, as if waiting for more, and gesturing me to carry on.

"I am your friend . .   Don't be scared . . ."

She looked on; I took her answer as a yes. I decided to go further. I took small, cautious steps towards her. She didn't hesitate. I reached over and touched her gently on her back. She stayed immobile, and kept on looking. My fear of her was soon gone, I petted and stroked her casually, and she meowed happily. It felt so good; I thought this might be a dream. Too bad Didi didn't get to experience this wonderful feeling with me.

I lifted her off the kitchen counter, and held her lovingly on my lap. Never in a million years had I imagined that she would accept me so lovingly on the very first day. I took her to my room and set her on the table. I moved away hastily, as my arms were hurting from holding her for so long. Something struck her as soon as she was set on the table. She began to scratch and hit the table and its contents. I was panicked at this sight. What if she woke someone up? I decided to get her out of the place soon. Maybe she didn't like the room or she was scared of me. Whatever the matter was, I didn't want to take any risk.

I gently picked her up but she refused. She began to scratch and bite my hands! I held her as tight as I could and went to the kitchen. I hoped that, after seeing the familiar sight of the kitchen, she'd calm down. But none of that happened. I went towards the window and tried pushing her out. We lived on the first floor and the distance between the ground and the window was a lot. I figured she could get down just the way she came up. I had also read somewhere that if a cat falls from whichever height, she lands on her paws and doesn't get hurt. But I wasn't sure. But the distance was manageable even if that statement wasn't true. She could go back just the way she came.

"Nitya . . . where are you?" Didi's voice seemed extraordinarily loud after this silent experience.

I hastily shut the window and poured myself a glass of water. Then carrying the water from the kitchen, I raced back to my room.

"I was just getting water." I said, I was shocked at how cheerful I sounded. I was glad I could think of an excuse so quickly.

"Oh . . . get some for me too . . . please . . . ?"

I went to the kitchen. On normal days I would have never done this for her but right now I wanted a reason to go back to the kitchen to see if the matter was settled or not. It had. Ginger was gone. Giving her the water, I turned back on my bed and pretended to sleep.

"Thanks . . ." Didi replied. I almost fainted then. I had never heard her say this word before. I had, but that was always sarcastically.

"Welcome . . . and good night." This made me realize that this *must* be a dream. Never in the world had Didi and I had such a mannered talk.

"So . . . excited?"

"For what?" I replied. I didn't want anything exciting right now. I wanted to have a normal day.

"The Maths quiz . . . it's to be held tomorrow. I am not taking part in it, but we get to miss a lot of classes to watch other quizzes . . ."

Dang . . . I am forgetting everything these days.

"Oh . . . I forgot. I am selected. That means I have the competition tomorrow! I haven't even studied!" I wailed.

"Who is the bookworm now? Huh? Ha-ha!" Didi's laughter rang in the eerie silence.

I decided to ignore this comment. I went to my study table and sat down. I picked up my book and turned open a random page. I decided I would study all night today . . .

CHAPTER-15

GUILTY CONSCIENCE

I woke up, but wasn't surrounded by the dull pink walls of my room but could feel the brown wood of the table . . . my study table.

I looked around; I was supposed to be studying all night, as if. I had fallen asleep on my table. I couldn't remember a thing of what I had studied last night.

"Wake up! Don't you want to see Ginger?" Didi . . . why was SHE getting so worked up? Why couldn't she just let me sleep!

Elder Sibling Rule #59: *They would never let you sleep. To balance it, don't let them sleep either.*

"No . . ."

"Why are you saying no? Come on! And don't worry, today this won't fail you . . . promise!"

I got up, trying to look excited. But I wasn't excited about seeing her, as I had already seen and touched her the day before.

As we were looking at the clips, a thought struck me. Didi would come to know about the encounter I had at night! I hastily went up to the computer, and pressed the delete button. It showed the delete confirmation window, and I heard Didi gaping behind me. I didn't stop. I pressed enter.

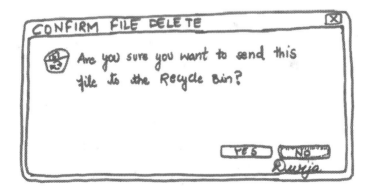

"What! What have you done! I hadn't even transferred it into the computer yet! I can't even get it back from the recycle bin!"

"Oops . . . Sorry . . . I was just having some fun!"

"Fun! Oh come on! All this time, I tried to do this for you. And you spoil the thing up for fun? I haven't slept well for days! What has gotten into you lately?"

For a minute, I felt bad about this. Why was I being so selfish? I mean, it was Didi who had helped me a lot in the past few days. It was because of her that I had come so far . . . Suddenly, it didn't seem right. I regretted what I was saying the moment after I said it, or did it.

"I'm sorry Didi . . . I know what I did was wrong . . . I am so sleepy and grumpy right now as I didn't get much sleep yesterday. I feel bad that I haven't even studied a bit for the quiz today! Everyone in my class thinks I cheated in the test. To top all the entire thing about Ginger . . . It seems so childish now, doesn't it? Who wants to do all this for a cat? I put a lot at stake for the cat."

Didi looked puzzled for a moment, and then she smiled. She smiled the way she does when she is hiding a secret. Her smile was ruthless, cunning and vindictive.

"Apparently, who was the one who fainted when she saw her? And I am just trying to help, I want some appreciation atleast. Okay then, do it on your own. Good night! Never ever talk to me again." Her voice was sugary sweet. I believe I mentioned that she is *Numero Uno* at such bubbly, fake voices.

I looked at Didi as she walked away. I felt a sigh of relief. Didi had got me this far, the rest I could manage. I didn't want her to see Ginger or touch or stroke her anymore, after what she did with me in school today, even though I had forgiven her. I looked at the book in front of me. It was still open on the page I had opened it the night before.

I got up and looked at the clock. It was 6 right now. Our school bus comes at 7:45 and we normally wake up at 7:30. I wanted to surprise my parents today. I went and started to get ready for school. I'll just leave the competition to luck.

CHAPTER-16

Mathswhiz Wonder

"Good morning students! The Math whiz competition is starting in a few minutes! We will start announcing the teams now. You can cheer for your respective classes and show your support!"

As cheerful as the host may have sounded, I was super scared. I hadn't studied, was super sleepy and wasn't getting an ounce of support from my fellow team members, not even from my own sister.

I realized that the host was starting to introduce the teams. The girl looked like she was just in 9th grade. I suddenly realized that she was the same girl who had pulled my cheeks the day before. When she turned to introduce my team, she gave me a small wink. I smiled. Atleast *someone* was smiling to me today . . .

"This is team 3, With Nitya Kumar as the team leader!" I didn't know I was leader. I guess the person with the highest score automatically became the leader. Trust me; I didn't want to be the leader.

She went on to introduce the rest of my team as I scanned the crowd for a smiling face. I wanted to see someone who would smile and motivate me during the quiz.

There was no one from my own class who was smiling at me. They were all glaring. I made a mental note to never ever look in other people's test papers even if you didn't intend to cheat. I looked at Nainika, who seemed to be busy talking to her friend. Suddenly my eye caught an arm waving. At first I wasn't sure for whom that wave was meant, but in a while I understood that the wave was for me. I looked to see who it was. To my surprise, it was that one person I didn't expect to see. It was Didi.

"What . . ." I mouthed at her.

She stopped waving and put both her hands to her ears. She was saying sorry to me. I looked on at her, clearly surprised. But then I realized how most of this is my fault and I should be the one saying sorry to her. I was the one who spoiled all her hard work by pressing delete. It was all because of my *guilty conscience.*

Elder Sibling Rule #65: *There are exceptions to every rule. Sometimes, they might just surprise you.*

"It's ok." I mouthed to her. I wished she would have apologized earlier; I wouldn't have to do this in front of the whole school. Well, almost. No one was looking at me or paying any attention.

She gave me an encouraging thumbs-up sign and I smiled. I tried to concentrate as the host explained the rules.

"Before I explain the rules to the participants, there is one big rule for the audience too. You cannot communicate or prompt the answers to the contestants. You cannot shout the answers even if the team is unable to answer, as the question will be passed on to the next team. Anyone found doing anything of this sort; his or her section's team will be disqualified immediately."

I thought about how Didi was in a different section than mine. Ha-ha, if she tried doing anything to humiliate me, her section will be disqualified . . . and that would do me good. I mentally laughed at how silly I was being.

"The rules for the contestants now . . ."

I gripped the edge of the table and squirmed in my seat. I was beginning to feel very nervous now. What if the toppers told the teachers that I was cheating of their paper even though I hadn't? I felt very scared at these possibilities. I shook myself to get rid of these bad, cruel thoughts.

"Contestants, here are your set of rules. There will be 5 rounds. You will be getting one question per round. If you cannot answer it or pass it to the other team, you will get 0 points. Each correct answer will give you 10 points and you will be given only 5 points for a passed question. Incase the question is being passed on and no team can answer it, then it will be an audience question and the audience can answer it. But you won't get any points for that. The lucky person in the audience will be getting a chocolate! Contestants, there is a blank sheet of paper in front of you in which you can write and do your calculations. There is also a pencil beside it which you can use. When I ask you a question, the team can discuss the question within itself and do the calculations. But you will be given only 30 seconds for that, so better be fast! Now, you guys are given 2 minutes in your team to discuss your team strategies and decide which person is going to announce the right answer in the team. This person will be known as the "Speaker". Only the speaker can say the answer on the microphone. Till then, I'm going to ask the audience some random questions. If you answer them correctly you get a chocolate! Teams, this is your cue to discuss strategies."

I turned over at my team. They were looking at me, questioningly.

I braced myself for what was coming.

"So . . . We call it a truce?"

I waited. No response. Just stares.

"Okay guys, look. I wasn't cheating or anything. I had already finished my paper till then and I was just looking around. I know that's a lame excuse but you will have to live with that for now. I don't want the team to lose just because we don't have unity among us. We have to bear each other, just for this. I mean, we all have waited so much for this moment, right? So it won't be correct if we spoil this by fighting. Come on, let's be a team and win this!"

I was shocked at my sudden burst of enthusiasm.

It was Rohit that spoke first.

"You're right. I agree with you. We all have waited and worked so hard for this. Now we are fighting like little kids. It's not right. What do you guys think?"

"Yeah, guys. Don't do this for me, do this for yourself." They were right. I really sounded like a teacher.

"Well, okay. I mean, we were wrong too by accusing you. Sorry." The toppers said. They looked like they were sorry too.

"It's ok. Now let's decide who is going to be the speaker."

"Seeing how you keep on speaking, let's make you the speaker." Rohit joked. Unfortunately, they took him seriously.

What? Me? NO!

"No, I don't think so . . ." I was scared out of my mind. I wouldn't speak the answers on the mike in front of the whole school!

"No ifs and buts. I mean, you got highest in English, right?" Rohit said, jokingly. I was certainly not enjoying even a single one of Rohit's jokes.

"Well, okay."

I wanted this to end as soon as it could. This already was making me so nervous.

The host was now back up on the stage, and she was holding cue cards in her hands. She finally spoke,

"I hope you guys have it all decided. We can start now. Also, there is a surprise bonus question in the end. The winner can get a 20 point bonus."

My heart soared. Even if we didn't win a few other questions, this bonus question was going to help a lot.

"First question for team A . . ."

I leapt up in my seat and listened intently.

"If it takes you 12 minutes to reach India Gate from a certain place, how much time will it take you to reach ¼ portion of the distance between that place and India Gate, considering the speed remains the same?"

Easy! My heart soared. If all the questions are going to be this simple, I would be able to answer each and every one of them. But I realized that they don't teach you fractions till grade 5. It could be hard for some . . .

"Umm . . . Can we discuss it?" The speaker from team A spoke, stammering and unsure of himself.

"Yes, of course you can. But remember, you have only 30 seconds!"

The team discussed and gave out the correct answer. And so did team B, I realized it was our turn now. I looked at my team members; they looked scared, but excited at the same time. I felt the same.

"Team C! Your question is . . . If A and B, both walk at the same speed towards each other in a straight route, which is of 10,000 meters, at what distance will they meet? Give the answer in kilometers. Take their speeds to be the same."

I smiled. I knew that the answer was 5,000 meters, which is just 5 kilometers. But still, for the sake of formality, I looked at the other members of my team. They all were looking at the paper with the pencil in their hands, but they were not writing anything. Rohit spoke to me in an urgent voice.

"None of us know the answer, but we also don't want to pass the question. What do we do?"

Before I could say that I knew the answer, the host shoved the microphone to my face. I heard the toppers whisper,

"Tell them you want to pass the question . . ."

I knew the answer and was sure it was correct. Even if it wasn't, we would get no loss as we would get 0 marks anyway. I decided we had nothing to lose.

"The answer is, 5000 meters which, when converted to kilometers, becomes 5 kilometers. This is the final answer."

I was shocked to see how confident I sounded on the mike. Normally I get shied away and my voice sounds meek. I heard Rohit gape. The toppers didn't say anything, but I could sense that they must be staring at me right now.

"That is the right answer! Good work team C! You win yourself 10 points."

I smiled triumphantly at the other members of my team. They seemed to smile at me. Finally, the toppers spoke.

"Sorry we thought you were the cheater. You really deserved to be the leader with the highest marks. You just proved it."

"Thanks. This was just a fluke. Trust me; the next rounds are going to be hard for me and easy for you!"

They smiled and we went back to concentrating on the other teams' questions. The fist two rounds passed smoothly and all the questions were being correctly answered by all the teams. When the third round started, all the teams were at 20 points. We were all neck to neck. This competition wasn't going to be easy.

"The third round is beginning now! The teams are all trying their best and I can already sense that this is going to be a tough match!"

I was happy; we were answering the questions well. Team A answered their question and got 10 points. When it was team B's chance, they decided to pass the question, and I realized that now we could get an extra 5 points! I listened as the host repeated the question and the toppers whispered the answer almost instantly. The next question was our own question which we solved with great help from Rohit. Team D was also able to answer their own question.

After round 3, the scores were-

Team A—30 points.
Team B—20 points.
Team C—35 points.
Team D—30 points.

We were happy that our team was leading, but I told them that anything could happen. After all, there were two more rounds and the bonus question, which was worth 20 points.

The fourth round was a tough one, it was about shapes. Even though shapes seem like a very easy topic, the questions were tough. We got a sense of that when Team A, who had answered all questions correctly till now, had absolutely no idea about what the answer should be. The question was passed on to team B, who managed to give out the correct answer, with a lot of discussion and calculations on their piece of paper. I thought they might be a strong competitor for us.

"Now, here comes the original question for Team B . . ."

I listened to the question. It was an easy one. I was sure they would be able to answer it. After what seemed like hours of discussion the speaker spoke.

"Umm . . . pass."

I looked on, dazed. The question was easy. As I wandered more and more into my thoughts, I realized that we were going to get the passed question. I looked at my team, ready for the discussion and a go at 5 extra points.

"Should we pass it too, Nitya?" Rohit asked, looking worried.

"No." I said, I couldn't believe I sounded so authoritative, which was so unlike me. They looked at me, amazed.

"I know the answer, guys."

"Well . . . if that's the case, we have nothing to lose." The topper spoke up. I made a mental note to look up their names, I felt awkward calling them 'toppers' all the time. I couldn't believe I was so oblivious to my own class.

I looked at the host and nodded. She handed me the microphone.

"The answer is a trapezium. It is an example of a quadrilateral with only one pair of parallel sides."

"That's the correct answer! Well done and your team gets 5 extra points. Good job!"

I beamed. I was doing *something* for the team atleast.

"Well done! Wow!" The topper spoke.

"Thank you. All thanks goes to me listening to my sister preparing for her examinations late at night. It comes to me as a lullaby."

121

"Wow." Rohit said. I thought, were they acting so goody-goody just because I was helping them win, or because they really thought I was good at answering the questions? Whatever the reason may be, I was glad I had stopped getting the cold shoulder.

The fourth team answered their question well. The results for the fourth round were put up.

Team A—30 points.
Team B—25 points.
Team C—50 points.
Team D—40 points.

I was happy that our team was leading. I thought team D was a good competition for us as it had answered all the questions, without passing any and not getting any passed ones, due to us answering them right.

"Now . . . we start the much awaited and nail-biting last round. This round is different. Maths is not always about calculations, is it? In this round, we will be giving one word or topic to any one member of the team. The other members will have to guess it. The Maths dumb-charades! This round cannot have any passes. But don't worry; you will get a chance to cover up in the bonus round. Now you will be getting one minute to pep talk your team and discuss who will be representing the team. Also, you can decide some code words or instructions! Get ready, teams!"

I turned back, anxious not to be the one who will be acting out the parts.

"So, who'll act? Please let this not be me again!"

"Then who will act?" Rohit asked.

"Any one of you . . ." I said, pointing at the toppers.

"It makes sense. You both are best friends and understand each other well. This will make it easier to guess it as you both know each other so well." Rohit said. I sighed a sense of relief. Rohit had a logical explanation. Whereas me . . .

The toppers looked at each other. Finally, one of them spoke.

"I'll do it." He said. He looked like he didn't want to, but *who gets what they want in life?*

We finished off discussing some key terms for *and, of, the*, etc. We had absolutely no idea about what kind of words we will be given.

"Time is up! I want to remind you, your chairs will be turned backwards when the other teams are performing. The currently performing team will be not using the microphone, so as the other teams do not get to listen. This way, each team has a fair chance."

Wow! They sure made rules very thoughtfully. The moment I think of a way to make it easier for our team, they spoil it.

"I have never seen a game show which is played with such kind of rules . . ." Rohit murmured, while turning his chair. I did the same.

The game started. I felt urged to pull my chair back and see what kind of acting the other teams were doing, what kind of words they got. But I laughed at these thoughts. That would disqualify our team.

"Psst . . . turn back your chairs, team C, it's your turn now."

We turned our chairs and the member from our team whom we selected to act for us, went up to the host. I felt butterflies in my stomach. After the host was done whispering, the boy turned to us and began his acting.

"Get ready . . . your time starts, NOW!"

He started to act. He made a horizontal line with his hand.

"Umm . . . horizon, sea?" Rohit said.

"No, that can't be. This is supposed to be a Maths word." I replied.

The other topper kept on gazing at his friend, not trying to participate in our discussion in any way. I tried to ignore him. I didn't have the time to argue. I would figure this out on my own.

Meanwhile, the actor kept on waving his hand like a line . . . sleeping line. What was he trying to show? A minus?

"The minus sign? Subtraction?" I was doubtful.

He waved his head in approval. But he still kept on repeating the sign. He balled up his hand in a fist, and then made the minus. He balled it in a fist and made the minus again, this time below the sleeping minus sign.

"Why are you repeating it so much?" I asked. I was getting frustrated. We had already guessed it, now shouldn't he switch to a different sign or symbol?

He nodded his head again. I sighed. This guy did surely not understand the game

"We have guessed it's a minus. Why are you repeating the sign so much?" Then it struck me. Repeated subtraction . . . Division!

"The division sign!" I shouted. He waved his hand, as if to tell me to go on. I felt relieved. Atleast he changed his action!

"Division, Umm . . . quotient? Umm . . . remainder?" He kept on waving his hand.

"Divisor, dividend . . ." I rattled on, saying everything related to division I knew.

"Right answer! Well done." I hadn't realized that the host was there, the audience was staring at us, and I was in a competition. I had forgotten everything for a split second.

I beamed. I hadn't studied much for this, but I was happy that I was doing so well. I just hoped that we are able to do well in the bonus round, or else we might even lose.

We turned back our chairs as the last team proceeded with their chance. I was sure that they would be able to answer it. I quickly calculated the scores in my mind.

Team A—40 points.
Team B—35 points.
Team C—60 points.
Team D—50 points.

I knew I shouldn't be too happy right now, as the 20 point bonus could change the game.

CHAPTER-17

SUSPENSE

I stared at the blank sheet in my hand. This was something I hadn't expected at all. Creative writing! I never knew Maths had creative writing. We were all supposed to write a 1 page story on the given topic. This bonus question was one of the worst rounds so far.

"Each player in the team will be writing the story individually. We will be collecting all the 16 stories and judging them. This might take some time, so the results will be out by the end of the day. They will also be put up on the bulletin board, where you can check the winning team."

This was very humiliating. I had thought this would be a Maths quiz, which turned out very well for us. But as the day is passing, the surprises were getting more stressing.

"The topic is, 'How I use Maths in my daily life.' You may start writing now; you will be getting 15 minutes only. The audience is now directed to leave and resume your classes. Please don't make a lot of noise, or else the participants might get disturbed."

The kids in the hall started to evacuate, the children making noise as they moved. I felt more relaxed, sitting in an empty hall and writing. I directed my eyes to the paper and began to write . . .

"Thank you all! This was a fun quiz." The host sounded as tired as we were, as she collected our sheets and we began to leave. Before we left, she handed each of us a small box with our names written on them. Seeing this as an opportunity, I looked at the name tags. The topper's names were Aryan and Abhimanyu. I took my box and tiredly started to walk back to my classroom.

"You really saved us from losing today, Nitya. We are sorry for the mean things we said to you." Aryan spoke. I couldn't believe he was apologizing.

"It's ok. It was a fun experience. Hope we make it to the school level. We would have to work very hard to achieve that." I couldn't help smiling at them.

"Yes, you're right. Let's race to the classroom!" Abhimanyu said, already starting to run.

"Hey! Wait up! You're *cheating*!" I shouted, running. Aryan and Rohit followed. This was turning out to be a good day. I hope the results go well too.

We reached class, panting. The class stopped writing and looked at us. Even the teacher looked at us and stopped teaching. Suddenly, the whole class started to cheer. The teacher smiled at us. Even though she was smiling at the whole team, I felt that the smile was meant especially for me. We returned to our seats amidst the cheering and hooting.

"Settle down class. They are tired too. Let them rest. You can talk to them in the next class, which happens to be recess." The teacher continued to write on the board and the students eventually started to write. After all heads were bent, I looked at the box in my hand.

It was a big box; I wondered what was in it. I opened it. Inside, was a sharpener shaped like a train's engine. It was the kind that you put the pencil in the hole and rotate the handle on the other end. I had seen it a lot on the TV. I looked up and saw that even the others were inspecting the memento that was given to us. I wanted to show this to Didi. I kept it back in the box and closed the box with the ribbon and carefully kept it in my bag. The bell rang and all four of us were surrounded by swarms of kids congratulating and asking questions. It felt good to be the center of attention for once.

"Nitya, you were amazing up there! You knew the answers to practically all the questions!" It was Nainika. I was glad she had finally broken the ice.

I smiled. "Ha-ha, my luck."

"What about the writing part? Who won?" Nainika asked.

"We don't know yet. The results will be out before the end of the day." Rohit said, pulling his fingers to form a cross and waving it towards the rest of the members of the team. We all did the same.

After the excitement and the questions had died down, everyone went to their respective groups and I was left alone as always. I didn't mind that, I was used to it.

"Nitya! Come here!"

I looked up to see Didi and her gang of friends standing at the door. She was waving at me, chocolates in her hand. A day or two ago, she was the one who told me to go away. Now she was here to meet me. This seemed fishy to me.

"Hello, Didi." I recognized the host of the quiz in Didi's gang.

"Look at all these chocolates! I answered all the questions that Swati put before us when you were discussing the strategies! Ha-ha."

"You did great in that competition Nitya!" The host, Swati, spoke up.

I blushed. "Thank you."

"Come on, I'll take you to the canteen! My treat!" Didi said, she seemed very enthusiastic today.

"Ok, let's go." I closed my lunch box and followed Didi. I had never gone to the other canteen where Didi usually frequented. There was a junior canteen in our building which I preferred to use. The big canteen was for the seniors and we all were very scared of the big, burly seniors.

"I don't want to go, Didi." I didn't feel well about going there.

"Why? Are you not hungry?" Didi replied, not being able to guess the real reason of my discomfort.

"No, I'm scared about the seniors. We have been told in class not to talk to them."

"Ha-ha. We seniors aren't **vampires**[12]. Come with us and don't worry."

I went with her to the canteen. It wasn't at all like I had expected. The seniors were standing in small groups and talking loudly. They weren't fighting or teasing people as I had been expecting them to do.

Didi took me to the main part of the canteen and told me to choose whatever I wanted. I never had such many options, as the junior canteen was restricted to only healthy food.

"I'll have a burger and a coke." I didn't want to have any other delicacy, as I wasn't able to understand what the other food items were. I saw a girl munching on a burger and thought it might just be the safest bet.

---

[12] **Vampires:** Mythological or folkloric beings who subsist by feeding on the life essence (generally in the form of blood) of living creatures.

"Okay. Let's order."

Didi and her friends went up to the counter and came back a minute later with food. Didi had got me the burger and coke I wanted and had ordered for a plate of momos for herself. I suddenly remembered my sisters craving for Chinese food.

"I think I should go back to my class and eat. I also have to complete the work which I left when the bonus round was on. Thanks for the treat!"

"No problem. Bye."

"See ya, cutie-pie!" Swati yelled, pulling my cheeks.

I rushed out. I didn't want to stay in there for a minute longer. The huge boys and girls, even though they looked sweet, made me want to stay away. I felt uncomfortable, a small little girl in this big, scary world.

I went back to my class and finished my food. Rohit came up to me and said, "The results are up. You want to go and check?" He seemed nervous to go alone.

"Aryan and Abhimanyu have already left," he added.

"Okay. Let's go." I finished the last bites of my burger and gulped down my beverage as fast as I could. I went out towards the main hall, wringing my hands nervously as I walked.

"Don't worry. Let's just pray," Rohit seemed very worried himself. He tried to put on a brave face.

If we win this, it would enable us to reach the State level and compete with the other schools. This thought was scary. I shuddered.

The scene in the notice board was scary. Around 20 children were shoving and pushing each other, trying to get a look at the paper. I spotted the toppers at the corner, trying to get in to look. There were children who didn't even take part in the quiz. What brought them here?

I shoved past the children and reached the front. I breathed deeply and looked at the paper in front of me.

CHAPTER-18

A New Friend

"The team which has made it to the next level is team C." I repeated this line till I was absolutely sure that this wasn't a dream or a mirage. It seemed so true, yet so unbelievable at the same time.

"Woo Hoo Nitya! We made it!" Aryan was jumping around, yelling.

"I can't believe it." Rohit gushed.

"Neither can I." I said, but I couldn't help smiling and feeling ecstatic myself.

We read the paper completely again and realized that we had to go meet the teacher in-charge immediately. We practically ran towards her table in the staff room.

"Good Afternoon, kids. Well done."

"Thank you, ma'am." We said in unison.

"That was a wonderful performance by your team. Now, I need to let you know that there will be a State level competition on 16th March. That is a good 3 months away. I want you to study hard. For your aid, we will be giving you some books to study from." She said, handing each of us a pile of about 8-10 fat books. They were as thick as my sister's Harry Potter's. The toppers were happy, but my eyes bulged out.

"If you don't mind, we were thinking of teaching all 4 of you. Will that be okay?"

The idea of a teacher teaching us was better than studying the whole set of books myself. But I knew, when do we get the time? There had to be a catch.

"We will be using some of your free periods to conduct extra classes. We might take away your PE class, music, art, etc. Don't worry about your grades, we will handle those. Your zero periods will be used too. Also, we will be holding regular stay backs on Tuesday and Thursday. Is that okay? Don't worry; the classes are going to be fun, as we won't be studying only from books, but through computer games, cards, etc. I am sure you all would enjoy them."

I looked at the others. They all looked at each other. This was turning out to be *damn* serious.

"Yes, Ma'am. That'd be fine with us." I replied. I loved Maths. I enjoyed learning it.

"Okay, great. We would make you a different time-table, and you can collect it from me first thing tomorrow morning."

We went back to our classes. The children were all bubbling with excitement that their class had won and the teachers were congratulating all of us. The day finished way too quickly. I wanted to go back home and sleep. I was so tired.

I went to the bus and looked for a seat. There wasn't any seat left. Usually I sit with Didi but she had her tennis stay backs today. I looked at the seats with only one person who might give me a chance to sit.

"You can sit here, Nitya." I looked up. I saw Divya sitting on an empty seat, beckoning me to come sit with her.

"Oh, Thanks Divya." I said, sitting. I was so tired that I was not going to let this chance go, even though all she is going to do is brag around all day.

"Where's Natasha?" I asked. I thought for a second why she was sitting in this bus. Was I in a wrong bus today?

"She doesn't go in this bus. What about you? Where is your sister?"

"She has some extra class today. I was wondering, how come I never noticed that you go in the same bus as me?"

She smiled, but the smile was nervous.

"I just shifted my house. I am going in this bus for the first time."

"Where are you living now? Isn't it fun? A new house, a new room . . ."

"I haven't seen my house yet. My mom is going to be waiting for me at the bus stop."

"How will you know which stop you have to get out on?" Divya had a busy mom. My mother would never leave me in a strange bus alone.

"The bus conductor will tell me. My mom talked to him already."

We talked to each other all through the bus journey. It was fun talking to her, she seemed so sweet.

"I have to go, my stop is next." I got up and collected my things. I saw the conductor wave at Divya.

"Divya *beta*, this is your stop. Come, your mother is waiting."

Divya got up and looked at me. Then she beamed.

"Wow! We have the same stop! This is good. Now you and I will ride the bus together everyday!"

We got down from the bus and went towards our mothers. I was happy to find that Divya's mother was talking to mine.

"Mom, meet Nitya. She is in my class at school." Divya said, hugging her mother.

I looked at her mother and smiled. She looked so sweet. I greeted her and shook her hand.

"Nice to meet you, Nitya. How are you?"

"I'm fine." I replied, looking at my mom.

"Mom, has the furniture reached?" Divya asked her mom.

"Yes. Let's go and see your new room! You can decide how you want to decorate it. The previous owners have the room painted a pretty purple colour for you already! Isn't that nice?"

"Wow! Nitya, will you come to my house with me? Let's decide how we want to decorate it!"

I was shocked. The day was full of surprises for me today. First the quiz, then the apology, Didi's unexpected treat and now Divya.

"Yes of-course! Nitya will love to go."

I stared at my mother. She never sent us to anyone's house without knowing them. And Divya had just shifted into the locality!

"You know what, Nitya? Aunty had been a very good friend of mine when we were in college. But we lost touch. Divya is in your own class, you both can become very good friends!" Mom seemed happy to have a friend she could talk to in our locality.

"I don't know your house, Divya . . ." The idea of we both becoming good friends was hard to digest.

"Our house is just next to yours! We live on the 2nd floor of the next building. You both can see each other everyday." Aunty said, smiling at Divya.

I suddenly remembered how the second floor had been empty since the last 2 months.

"But how come you never mentioned this in school?" I had never known this would happen.

"I didn't want anyone to know. I told Natasha and a few other friends about it. But we both rarely talk in school. I didn't even know where we were shifting, how big the house was, etc. So I didn't want to look like a dumbo and say that I was shifting and I don't know where." She laughed. Her laugh was so carefree, so innocent. I felt like we both might just get along.

"Are we both going to stay here all day? Let's go!"

I followed her to her house, which was, as aunty had said, very close to ours. I looked at the empty house. Aunty had already started to unpack items and setting up the house. There were labourers all around, holding beds and closets.

"This is your new room, Nitya! I'll send a man along to help you put the bed and move things around. If you have any problem, just call me. And don't touch any heavy item by yourself."

"Okay mom." Divya said and sat down on the middle of the empty room. The room was big. It had a pink ceiling fan and purple walls. The door was white in color.

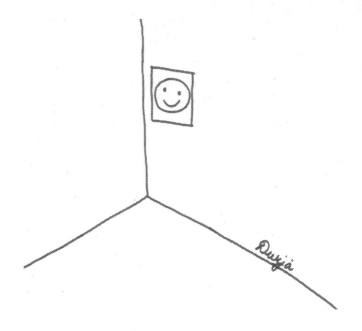

"Where do you think we should put the bed?" Divya asked.

"Well, what all items are there that we have to put?" I wanted to know what all was there.

"There is a bed, a closet, a study table desk and a cabinet made of glass which has to be hanged on the walls." She said, thinking.

"There are also some wooden shelves which used to be above my bed, but I want to change their position. Every morning, my day always started by banging my head on the wall!"

We both laughed. She wasn't as mean as I had expected her to be. She was becoming a good friend. I wonder why she never was this sweet to me in school.

"You know what, Nitya? I've always been so jealous of you."

"Why is that so?"

"I'm an only child, so I often feel lonely. You are so lucky to have an elder sister you could play with all the time."

"Trust me, they are never fun. Try living with one. All they do is fuss about their clothes, their hair . . . Always talk on the phone and text message people. They never want to play with you. They don't like the things that you want to watch on TV, and always put on some English serials that you can't understand. They stay on the computer all day, socializing. Whenever you want to understand a certain topic from them, they always make up an excuse about how busy they are."

"Can't you tell your mother about it? She would tell your sister to help you and talk well with you." She seemed to have a counter statement to every accusation I had thought up in my mind.

"Hah! They are also wonderful actors. They act like an angel in front of mom. Sit down on the table and study. But if you pick up their textbook there is always another novel or phone hidden there."

"Big sisters are funny!" Divya said laughing. I never knew she was such a sweet and funny girl. I guess life is full of surprises.

"NO! They are a pain!" I said. We both laughed till our stomach hurt. We doubled up, still laughing.

"Yes, do you need any help with the furniture?" A man with torn and mud-stained clothes appeared on our door.

We told him how we want to put the furniture, and he did exactly that.

We both were having so much fun that I didn't realize that it was seven in the evening and my mom had come to take me home. I was happy and skipped all the way to my own house.

"So . . . did you have fun?" Mom asked me.

"Yes! It was so much fun! I'll tell you everything."

I told her everything. About the quiz, the sharpener, Divya . . . all this time, she listened with rapt attention. Taking in all that I said . . .

CHAPTER-19

BUSTED!

That night I had forgotten about Ginger and the encounter I had with her the night before. It seemed like so much time had passed since then and so much had happened. I lied down on my bed and pulled the covers over me. But I couldn't sleep. I looked at Didi. She was already fast asleep. I got up and went towards the kitchen for a glass of water. To my surprise, someone was sitting there and waiting for me. It was none other than my little feline friend, Ginger.

"Hey there, cutie pie!" I said, extending out my arms. To my astonishment, she leapt in my arms.

She meow-ed happily and I stroked her, she was just so cute.

"What is happening here?" I was interrupted by a sleepy sound.

I whirled around to see my maid standing there, with a broomstick in her hands.

"I was umm . . . nothing . . ." I couldn't think of an excuse. Ginger was still in my arms and was staring curiously at my household help. I was caught red-handed. Or if I say so myself, Ginger-handed.

"Aww . . . is that your little friend?" She came forward to stroke Ginger, who turned away and snuggled deeper in my arms.

"You scared her!" I said jokingly.

"She can't get scared from me . . . I know her!"

"You know her?" I didn't want her to be anyone else's cat. I loved her.

"Yes. I had a cat once, her name was Rani. Rani gave birth to three little kittens over a year ago. That was the time I came here to work in your house. I brought Rani and her kittens along with me. Your mother doesn't like cats, so I had to leave them out in the open! Now see, she has come back to you!"

"That's great! Then you must know a lot about cats. Tell me how to take care of them!"

My maid's happy expression turned sour.

"Your mom won't allow a cat in the house. That too a black cat." She said grimly.

"Why won't she? Ginger is such a cute kitty!" I stroked Ginger, and she sneezed. I laughed. She was 2 feet of unadulterated cuteness.

"Yes she is, but cats aren't considered a good omen."

"Why is that so?" I couldn't think of anyone who could reject such a cute little animal.

"Because cats are a major superstition!" She said, getting irritated by the second.

I suddenly remembered the black cat superstition.

"Oh! What about her?" I asked, pointing to the little bundle of fur in my arms.

"She has to go." My maid said sourly, putting emphasis on '*she*' and making a flicking motion with her hands, as if she didn't care.

I reluctantly sent her out of the window and closed the latch. She was still on the window sill, before I knew it, a tear escaped my eye.

I went towards my room and slept. Dreaming about going to a pet store to buy things for my Ginger.

CHAPTER-20

CHUBBI

The next morning I was in an amazing mood. It could be due to my victory the day before, the surprising friendship with Divya or Ginger from the night before.

"Get ready fast! You are going to get late!" mom was yelling at the top of her voice, breaking my train of thought.

"Yes, yes! I am coming!" I stuffed books into my bag and hastily reached the front gate.

"Where's Didi?" I asked. It wasn't fair that she was yelling at me if Didi was still getting ready.

"She left. She had an important exam today."

We went towards the bus stop hurriedly, only to find that the bus had left.

"Now we will have to drop you by car!" mom said exasperatedly as she began to walk towards the parking lot.

The journey in the car was quiet. As we were nearing the school, a cat crossed the road. Mom stopped the car.

"Mom! We're getting late!"

"A cat has crossed our way, let someone else cross the way first."

Luckily for us, a rickshaw crossed the path, not paying attention to why a car had suddenly halted in the middle of the road.

"You really don't like cats, do you?" I said, before thinking.

"I don't hate cats. But there are a lot of superstitions related to cats. A cat's crying is also not considered a good omen."

"But you always said that we shouldn't believe in superstitions. Then why do you follow them yourself?" I was going to set this matter straight, once and for all.

"I don't believe in them. But other people do. It doesn't harm to be a little more cautious than usual, even if it seems a little silly. You know what they say, 'Better be safe than sorry.'" Mom's argument made sense.

Given mom's current opinion to cats, Ginger could never be accepted in the family.

"Come on, Nitya! We have to attend our extra class." Abhimanyu said, the moment I entered the class.

Extra class was nice. The teachers were joking around and trying to make it seem like an interesting class, which it surely was.

I decided right there and then, that I have to do something about this matter. Ginger and I were becoming good friends, I didn't want anyone to come to know and scold me for lying all this time. I wanted to tell them myself.

I couldn't tell mom or dad. At least not right now. The only option I had left was Didi. I would tell her in the bus.

"Didi, I need to talk to you. Can I sit here?"

"Yes, come on." Looking at my serious expression, Didi gave in immediately.

I filled her in about everything. She listened patiently.

"That's cool, but I can't help you on this."

"Why?"

"Tell me something I *can* do, Nitya. What can I do? I can't persuade mom. And you want her as a pet? Have you seen anyone with a pet cat? It's OK in other countries, but I don't think this would work here. If you want we could get you a pet dog."

"I don't want a pet dog!" I said, fuming. They can't replace Ginger with a dog. And only because of an old wives tale!

"Nitya, will you come here for a minute?" I didn't realize I was standing in the middle of the bus. I turned around to see Divya motioning me to come and talk to her.

"What is it?" I asked.

"You can come sit here with me. Let's talk."

I carried my backpack and sat beside her.

"Can you come to my house today?" She asked, gazing at me expectantly.

Didi was already irritating me. I needed a break.

"Yes I would. Is all your furniture set?"

"A little bit is still left . . . but my room is okay. I want you to meet someone."

"Who?" I asked.

"My dog Chubbi! She is a white poodle."

"I didn't see her the first day I came to your house. Did you just buy her?"

"No . . . We left her with my grandmother as we were moving. She just got back this morning."

I smiled. But I felt sad. Divya had a pet. My pet had a whole array of superstitions following her anywhere she went.

Chubbi was, as Divya said, the cutest poodle ever. She was white and fluffy. She wasn't that kind of dog you were scared of. She leapt up in Divya's arms the moment she entered the house.

"She is so cute! Like a little ball of fur . . ." I said, as I held her in my arms and stroked her furry head.

That day at home I decided to tell everyone about my wish. I called everyone in the living room and said I wanted to hold a "Family Meeting". The moment I saw all of them enter and sit down, in mock discipline, I felt scared and my legs began to shake.

CHAPTER-21

FAMILY MEETING

"What important topic do you want to discuss with us?" Didi asked, looking all serious. But as soon as mom and dad looked away, she gave me an evil smirk, as if to say, *'Ready for some drama? Bring it on!'*

Elder Sibling Rule #21: They love some drama . . . especially if you are the one who causes it.

"I want to say that I recently won the school quiz . . ."

"And we are proud of you for that, *beta*." Dad said.

"I want a pet. I want someone I can take care of." I blurted, all me pre-prepared speech went down the drain.

"What breed of dog do you want?" Mom asked, getting excited. Mom loves dogs. She had one before, but she never got a new one when her older dog, Romeo, died. My mom had been a great Shakespeare fan, hence her dog was named Romeo.

"I don't want a dog." I said. Why do they assume that a dog is the only kind of pet?

"A bunny? That would be so cute! A fluffy little bunny . . ." Didi said. What kind of brilliant acting was this? I looked at her. She smiled. She really did deserve an Oscar for this performance.

Elder Sibling Rule #39: *They are award deserving actors. Better, Oscar deserving actors.*

"No." I wanted them to think of it themselves.

"A hamster?" Mom said.

"Dad, mom, listen to me." Didi said, giving me the cut-it-out look.

"My little sister here wants a pet *cat*" She put extra emphasis on the word cat.

"A cat?" Mom seemed as if I had proposed to have a T-rex as a pet.

"Not just any cat. I know which cat. She is in our locality and I have been feeding biscuits to her for a long time and since a few days, she has been even coming into my lap."

"I don't think that's possible . . ." dad had started to negotiate already!

"But I love her. Didi helped me get her. She loves Ginger too!"

"No I don't! I just helped you to see her. I didn't tell her to come in your arms. I certainly didn't tell you to have her as your pet."

"But mom . . . nothing makes sense . . ." I was on the verge of crying but I controlled myself.

"It's not about superstitions. A cat needs open space. We can't confine her in the house like a dog. Have you seen cat food anywhere? We can't catch mice and feed her!" Dad said, trying to lighten up the mood. I laughed.

"We would have said yes, but who would have taken care of her? Taking care of dogs will be comparatively easier as many people have dogs and could help us. No one would take care of a cat for us if needed."

I knew what they said was right. I hugged all of them. I wanted Ginger, but I wouldn't do it if my parents didn't allow it.

That night I closed the window to prevent Ginger from getting in. I knew what I was doing was wrong, but it was good for her in the long run.

Days passed. I studied day and night for the Maths quiz. I went to Divya's or she came to my house almost everyday. Believe it or not, she had become my best friend.

All was going fine, until I got that unexpected call from Divya.

Divya

"Hello?" I said.

"Nitya? It's Divya."

"Oh! Hi Divya, what happened?" I heard what she said and my eyes were wide open in amazement and shock.

CHAPTER-22

GINGER

I rushed over to Divya's house with my mom. It was somewhere mid-February and the night weather was beautiful.

"Come on in, Nitya. Hello aunty." Divya hastily exchanged greetings and pulled me towards her room. I went in to see a very tired Chubbi in her bed, with small bundles of fur all around.

"Oh my god! So many cute puppies!" My heart melted at their site. I picked up one of them. They were all white in colour, ditto copies of Chubbi.

"That's an amazing surprise!" I said, as Divya stroked Chubbi.

"There is one more surprise, but I would need your mom's permission. My mom is talking to her right now."

We rushed out to the living room, where Divya and my mom were sitting on the sofas and chatting.

"Mom, did aunty give permission?" Divya asked.

"Yes I did. That's so sweet of you!" My mom spoke up.

"Sweet for what? What permission? Can someone please tell me?" I asked with mock anger.

"We are letting you keep one of the puppies!" Divya shouted.

I stood there, stunned. I looked at mom. She smiled and nodded her head.

"Come; let's choose the cutest one for you!"

We went in and began to examine the cutest pup. One caught my attention. It was pure white, with a gingerish coloured mark on her forehead. I picked her up.

"You pick that one? That's so cute! What are you going to name her?"

I didn't hesitate. "Ginger"

That night I didn't sleep. I had Ginger sit on my lap and fed her milk. She reminded me a lot of my cat, Ginger. But I loved her all the same.

Days passed by and Ginger became more and more familiar with the members of the family and the house. I forgot all about the Ginger who used to come to meet me at night. The window never got opened again, and even if it did, I didn't get to know.

"Wake up, aren't you excited? It's the last day of school for you! Vacations start tomorrow!" Didi was sitting on her bed and yelling.

It was the end of February and it was the last working day of school. The exams were starting tomorrow but only for 5th grade and above. The rest, including me, had the last day of school today. I was glad it was the last day but sad that Didi had her exam tomorrow.

I got ready, fed Ginger and left for school. Last day fever was on, there were parties and fun, no one wanted to study, and the teachers didn't want to teach us either. But teachers had to give us homework!

"It's the last day of school! Why are we getting Homework?" Rohit asked. His habit of queer questions was still just as prevalent.

"It is something to help while away your time while the other classes have exams. We don't want you to watch TV all day and disturb your siblings, who have exams. The new teacher you will have for the next year will grade them. Don't have such sad drooping faces, it is a fun homework! Nainika, come and help distributing the homework sheets with me."

I had my school level MathsWhiz Competition in two weeks; I didn't want to do homework.

The homework given to us was rather easy though. There were some worksheets and assignments. But there was this one that caught my eye.

"Awaken the author in you! Write a book on any topic of your choice. Get creative! Take help from your parents, siblings and friends."

That day at home, I asked Didi about what I should write my book on, while stroking Ginger in my lap. She was growing fast, but I still loved her immensely. Didi was studying hard for her exam the next day.

"Why don't you write it about Ginger? Both the Gingers? That would be quite interesting . . ." I liked that idea. She went back to her books.

I started writing my book the very next day. It took a lot of hard work. Everyone was supportive of me. I am thinking about getting it published. I've even thought of a name for it.

'The World from the Eye of a Child'

Elder Sibling Rule #01: They love you more than you could ever imagine.